LEAVES
of
NARCISSUS

LEAVES
of
NARCISSUS

Somaya Ramadan

☙

Translated by Marilyn Booth

The American University in Cairo Press
Cairo ☙ New York

English translation copyright © 2002 by
The American University in Cairo Press
113 Sharia Kasr el Aini, Cairo, Egypt
420 Fifth Avenue, New York 10018
www.aucpress.com

First paperback edition 2006

Copyright © 2001 by Somaya Ramadan
First published in Arabic in 2001 as *Awraq al-narjis*
Protected under the Berne Convention

Dar el Kutub no. 15640/06
ISBN-10: 977 416 058 4
ISBN-13: 978 977 416 058 5

1 2 3 4 5 6   12 11 10 09 08 07 06

Designed by Andrea El-Akshar/AUC Press Design Center
Printed in Egypt

To Yehia and Yasser

TRANSLATOR'S NOTE

When I was asked to translate *Leaves of Narcissus*, pleasure mingled with concern about the ramifications of translating the art of an author who is herself a skilled translator, and who has rendered Virginia Woolf in Arabic! Yet the process of creating a new text, this English-language novel, yielded an entirely pleasant collaboration and rendered an existing friendship stronger and deeper. I am grateful to Somaya Ramadan for her trust and for her gentle and perfect suggestions, while I remain responsible for infelicities or errors. Together we have gone where the novel would take us, and those who compare the Arabic novel and this English novel will find that their paths diverge in some particulars, though not in trajectory or destination.

Somaya Ramadan's fictional universe is wrapped round in layers of texts, spoken, printed, acted, filmed, told, and retold. Quotations from English-language print sources include the following: Thomas Flanagan quotes William Shakespeare's *Henry V*, Act III Scene 2, Macmorris's speech, as an epigraph at the start of his study *The Irish Novelists, 1800–1850* (New York: Columbia University Press, 1959);

the second quotation from *Henry V* is from the immediately preceding speech by Fluellen, also quoted by Flanagan: "I think, look you, under your correction, there is not many of your nation . . . ." Flanagan notes that Macmorris is the only Irishman whom "Shakespeare brings . . . onto his stage" (p. 3). The "long-legged fly" comes from the poem of that title by William Butler Yeats. And the reader will have the pleasure of locating other instances of Ramadan's intertextual universe.

LEAVES
of
NARCISSUS

It Might Be

The instant before submission is the most difficult of moments. This might be the secret to its vital attractiveness—the irresistible finality of it. The edge of resistance, a breaking point, when your being has stretched itself to its utmost and your consciousness has spun itself thin, tensile, to the finest and most transparent thread. The chasm before you is featureless: absolutely new, wholly defiant to all powers of imagination. Is it something like this that people sense as they are led to the gallows?

It might be. Some sort of hope might linger, accompanying them all the way to the vanishing point, inside the abyss. The only difference is that those people are led against their will. It must be more merciful that way. It must be that despair yields them to death, and so everything ends there. Or do they go on hoping until the end has come? The difference is that the end does come.

The pill is barely inside my mouth when I spit it out. Here it is, they whisper, just a tiny disk, and then you'll sleep so soundly! That's all you're required to do. And they *do* require it: my friends, my family. The nearest relations are arranging a kind little conspiracy after which *you will sleep so very soundly*! Negotiations commence and I exhaust the conspirators. My senses are perfectly focused. I note the tiniest shift in timbre is my own deliberate choice, for music is wholly in the timbre. Before my very ears, they transform themselves from one tone to another—and they take on brighter, sharper outlines. Their eyes gleam and smolder. Their bodies fill the space more densely now, even though they are weakened by exhaustion. Their eyes are ringed by dark halos, as though outlined in kohl. All of them, my relations, have become angels—the messengers of lonely death. They mass themselves into a single front while I, on my own, resist. The chemistry of my whole body is primed, my mind is sharply awake, charged to the maximum by the electricity of clarity, consuming its neurons in flash after flash through the brain's interior corridors where the truth behind appearances materializes in sharp bright relief; and where memory, today, is crystalline: they cannot kill you for then they will become murderers. They mean only to be assured that you, at your own bidding, will enforce the verdict upon your very own person.

"A tiny pink pill, and then you'll sleep forever, and your suffering will end."

Beginnings, being beginnings, change constantly, change every time. I do not know at what point the hubbub starts to take over my brain, my mind, my thoughts, my self. In this murky clamor, I cannot make out individual voices. Gradually the din extends its dominion, capturing the hours in which I normally sleep, annexing one hour and then the next until slumber and nothingness become synonymous. Malady and medicine, poison and antidote: like most things, they come in pairs and arrive simultaneously. Then I'm afraid. Who goes into oblivion of her own volition? Sometimes I deceive them. I make them believe I've swallowed it. When they rejoice I am sad. For hearts soften in sorrow, and sympathetic tenderness replaces cagey readiness, and overwhelms the requisites of self-defense. When my heart softens, they are transformed. The intense blackness that ringed their eyelids vanishes, and the tonalities of their voices change. The resonance of deception disappears from the word-scale and they all become angels: merciful, sympathetic, loving angels. What's another name for the angel of death? Who is his counterpart? Or is the angel of death simply another image of mercy, and another way to name it? Still they remain, ranged in a single front, like the teeth of a comb, completely in accord, the way people with a certain directed inner knowledge agree upon one matter even if they disagree on all else.

No difference in opinion among the wise will cool this generous warmth that flows among them now. They have agreed in loving kindness and trustful affection. They do what they do for a reason I cannot grasp. All I am sure of is that their intentions are good and sound, and that individual, personal, lonely death—my death, mine— is attributable to a higher wisdom; a higher good more lasting than I can be, a good more enduring, perhaps, than all of humankind. It must be so. Or else, how could anyone have ever yielded to such a fate?

I swallow the minute pink pill. Slowly, infinitesimally, the presentiments of death infiltrate and gradually begin to take over my body. A hard, suppressed shudder sweeps through me from the tips of my toes, culminating in an orgasm more intense and slower than anything I have ever experienced before, followed by another, and another. Wave after wave in the same tempo and the same steady strength. When the clutching and releasing finally die out and numbness engulfs my head, I'm so very sure that I have died, and so I give witness in a clear voice, just as they have taught me: that the kingdom of God is upon us, that there is no god but God . . . and the wise people clustered around me smile, contented in their grace. And I am peaceful at last, and submission prevails over all:

I bear witness that I have done all that was within my power. That I have resisted with all the will I possessed, that I clung fiercely up to that ultimate moment, even as I saw my mind hovering, circling away, and that I did not despair. If I remained without understanding, it was not because I spared any effort, but rather because good is vaster than my grasp, as is evil. And you, Lord, you who vanish and reappear like a trickster, conning me with your exquisite beauty: I see you, then I don't see you; and I seize fiercely on your manifestations: the trees and the mountains, flowers and humanity. When I do not live you as a harsh beauty in my very bones, a life filled to overflowing, replete in every cell; when the hideous cement-block buildings obscure you from my range of vision, and the abominable voices of microphones take over your melodies in my ears, and I no longer see the sky for the smoke that spills from garbage fires: it is then that I hold mulishly to faith in people, the children of your tears, the very lips of your laughter, and the steely, tender gleam of your kind cruel eyes. It is then that I can sympathize with my own plight, faced as I am with passing illusory judgment.

In that instant I am a little girl—no, I am all little ones in a single little girl's body. As I prepare myself for death, a little body, this one or that, or all of them in one, become one with me, inseparable; and I am faced with an awesome, fearful process. I must free them one from the other, and all from the inner spaces of my body and spirit. My self, upon which that voracious, duplicate, multiple devil feeds: she is me and she is not me. I command her as though I were an exorcist knowledgeable in the talismans and amulets that free suffering bodies from evil spirits. Under my breath, under the threat of immense danger, every cell in my body quivers; I must kill her and preserve my own soul.

Souls depart from bodies the way a streamer of silk is first scratched and then rent as it moves along a surface of splintered glass. How can I allow her to pass and endure her death rattles, and not die along with her? It is a terrible risk, but *they* encourage me. Now their faces are etched in the features of benevolent conspirators. A harsh, hard, cruel benevolence, for they, too, know that she might kill me and live, *she might*. Or, that we might die together. I summon all of my courage and I accept the terror of this peril; I set down my very life as a wager, death or survival. There is no one here to protect me, no friend, today; only a world that has lost all preferences and alliances, that stands witnessing us—witnessing me, witnessing her—as we struggle. *Her*: she might be this one of the pair, or perhaps she's the other one. She might transform herself in the familiar ways she does, to dupe me by becoming both at once. Killer or killed, I command her:

Di—ana!
Die—I—*ana*!
Or, am I saying:
Die Amna!

A LESSON IN
RECKONING SUMS

She loses her temper, loses it completely. Her small, angular face reddens so spectacularly that I can see the soft dark hairs rimming her stern mouth. Beneath those tightly set lips run a pair of arcs, permanently etched lines of prolonged anger and bitterness in a marble face. Miss Diana, Greek spinster, teaches sums and algebra to the hapless daughters of the bourgeoisie. She is always garbed in mourning, and often she loses her temper.

"You're stupid," she snaps, in English.

Her hand shoots out to clutch a dangling lock of hair atop the small forehead, closing her fingers around it. Her fist yanks the head down sharply onto the glass of the dining table. The Czech crystal is shaved and rounded at the edges, perfectly meeting the solid cedar wood, carved out of a single trunk: a hard, solid block. Miss Diana's cheeks collapse inward and the whiteness of her skin all but reveals her very jawbones, carved as they are to precision. Contrasting with her ivory pallor, her short hair appears blacker and glossier than it really is. She has a nervous disposition and she is quick to anger. And she is passionate about numbers.

I raised my hand to touch my hair. I didn't feel the slightest pain. My head had simply withdrawn, absented itself, gone to sleep. Denial is the only way to rescue pride. For a little person of hardly ten years to keep herself from crying, in such a scenario, is a spontaneous reaction, though perhaps not seemingly a natural one. The girl is not certain of the nature of her sin. And the accusation is difficult to parry, for she truly does not understand how to reckon these sums. But to all appearances, her face does not reveal the depth of internal confusion brought on by the shock of a skull's collision with the crystal that protects the dining table. No indeed, for that face displays complete unconcern. This blank demeanor was the only line of defense open to her, the sole permissible form that rebellion could take, the only manner in which to preserve precious self-esteem. Cut the ties and banish the world. And when her father enters smiling, exhibiting his customary optimism, Miss Diana pours out her complaint.

"Your daughter claims not to understand. I know perfectly well that if she really wanted to understand, she would. Your daughter has a head of stone."

The smile disappears from her father's face, and she can sense the anger rising, filling the space between them. So he, too, holds her responsible for failing to understand. If he didn't, wouldn't his voice rise to protest what this fretful, neurotic woman has said?

The crystal on the dining table has splintered. As is the wont of glass no matter how smoothly polished or thick, the crack first appears modest, restricted to a narrow area, simple and small. Quickly, though, it thrusts forward, like a stream of water painfully negotiating its own course across the ground, and then—faster and faster—it branches out into many tiny ravines until it overspreads a remarkable breadth of crystalline surface.

"Do you see?" she snaps, getting ready to leave, putting her pens and the ruler and gum eraser methodically in her briefcase, in a manner that cannot but display her well-ordered character: tidy, practical and swift; all signs of the intellectually gifted according to the culture of this little house.

"Now have you seen? Her head is harder to budge than the crystal."

Nothing cuts diamonds but diamonds; only iron can file down iron, but glass breaks when hit by stone. No one took any interest in repairing the cracked glass on the dining room table. Its web of splinters long remained, visible to everyone, irrefutable evidence of the sort of brain that inhabited that head. A mind incapable of simple calculations, when solving mathematical problems is prime evidence of the mind's flare, swiftness, and clarity. All of the other things—the stories, novels, films and plays, history and poetry and drawing and photography—are mere diversions, enjoyable pastimes for those who know their sums. But that is allowable only after they have finished with the important matters of the world, the serious things. These "diversions" are my sole place of sanctuary, a place where one can make a world for oneself in which the glass on dining room tables does not crack or splinter.

But even when cushioned away in my sanctuary, I remained aware that from glass *they* might craft great, isolating bells by which to distinguish those who know sums from those who do not. Reckoning, then, is the great and hallowed criterion. So, I taught myself the only reckoning possible at the time. Reckoning is the Day of Reckoning, as in our religion lessons. On the Day of Reckoning, people must walk along a single hair's breadth without losing their balance, and in the end those who have been good fall into Paradise while the ones who have been evil topple into the Fire. I became determined neither to fall one way, nor to topple the other. And every day became a Day of Reckoning. But of course *they* were not aware that I understood then, that decimals and fractions do not afflict glass and crystal. What shatters glass and crystal are rocks and stones. They did not realize that I had begun to care for the boulder that filled me, such that I would sleep and sense the weight of my brain on the pillow. I would run my fingers carefully over my face, probing its features, knowing that as I slept it would change into the face of a statue carved from stone: a Medusa. Upon awakening, I would be instantly afraid for my eye to fall upon them. And so I no longer looked anyone in the eye. I thought they would not notice. Until I learned that all along they'd thought I was so shy I could not look anyone in the eye. How they came to that conclusion they never told me.

The other half of the time an anticipatory thrill fills my whole being. Something extremely exciting is about to happen, I'm sure of it!

Whole days pass and nothing happens. Nothing—only this constant state of expectation mingled with agitation. The days are ordinary. I awake as late as seven thirty since school is only a few steps away. I brush my teeth and comb my hair and knot my tie and shove my feet quickly into my soft, black shoes. Sandwiches and tea are waiting for me on a table in the kitchen. I swallow my breakfast and kiss her rapidly, Nana Amna; and my mother is somewhere in the background. When I open the door Amna appears and stands with me until the elevator arrives. I don't hear a sound from my mother, but Amna is clear and forceful.

"Bye bye! *Bye* now, go *on*, good riddance!"

The days are ordinary, so why then does my heart beat so? Something very exciting is about to happen. And then—nothing. Only undivided attention, precision, care in all things, no more than that, ever, and no less. I walk to school. The curb of the pavement has enchanted me. It promises the excellence that comes after sufficient practice. It is a single unending pavement, that leads in a grand half circle, from the entrance of our building to the school. Just one sidewalk, and at the end you always find the school and *Amm* Uthman, the enormous Nubian doorman. I reach school, walking on the edge, carefully balancing my steps. In school I write my lessons with utmost care, in a precise hand. I do not permit myself to use an eraser. At the end of every class period the teacher scolds me for being slow, and doesn't offer any praise for the clean look of my work or the orderliness of the page, nor does she seem to notice the lack of mistakes. The antidote for that terror that wells up suddenly, and seizes my being, is vigilant caution and an eye to the minutest detail. This fear that overwhelms me is, I'm certain, a fear of error; and possibilities for error are limitless. *They are utterly without limit.* And no one notices, no one remembers. Except me.

Every cell in the body grows weak under the pressure of this frighteningly rapid movement around the nucleus. Her body all but dissolves and scatters under the consuming force of this fuming activity.

She returns home, accompanied by the same fear that had walked out the door with her as she left home in the morning. On her return journey, specifics alter. She can walk the curb only the length of two pavement sections, and then she falters: a sense of failure saturates her. Her heart beats faster and she imagines her cells consuming themselves. In her ear rings the voice of Miss Cleaver reading Wordsworth, submerging the girl in the bewitching music of the words; her heart pounds to the rhythm of the poem, pounds, and then pounds faster— but it is not clear why. She's almost running at top speed to reach the shore of safety. There she'll find her mother and Amna and *Amm* Abduh the cook, and they will understand. Two by two, she leaps up the stairs into the building and pulls open the door to the elevator with a trembling hand. As she reaches the third floor her spirit sinks down through her legs, and into her feet. She rings the bell. Now fear is stronger than caution, and the girl kicks the door with her foot so they will hurry. When Amna opens the door her face is grim, unsmiling, knotted in a horrid frown. Her eyes betray anger, even bitterness. Her voice rises, accusatory without apparent reason:

"Get in here. Change those clothes. Wash your face. Hurry up! Your mother is at the hairdresser's and she's left me in a fix, and folks will be here any minute for lunch."

I apologize to her.

For what? Why did I apologize? I don't know now, except that it is very important for voices not to be raised. Calm and quiet are very important, for without them something might happen when I am not paying attention.

I throw my arms around Amna's neck entreatingly, but she pushes me away and her frown intensifies.

"Now *shaykha*, go on now," she says in a loud voice. "None of *you* has anything to plague you . . ."

I swallow it all in a single gulp and go off to change my clothes as the ringing in my ears ascends and redoubles. She didn't say a single thing that called for an answer, did she? I wait, and I watch.

After a short while her mother arrives, and now all is commotion: final preparations must be made before the guests arrive. Her mother is in the "office" filling the flower vase hurriedly but with perfect symmetry and precision. Her mother is breathing slightly hard and at first does not notice her daughter in the room. When she does see the girl, she asks: "Is that really the only pullover you have? Can't you put on another one?"

Her head is swathed in a ringing that wells up from somewhere within to block her ears against outside sounds, and she is not aware that when she feels her body consuming its life span with the speed of lightning or perhaps even faster, and she can barely stand it, that she is alone in this. She cannot bear it all. She is the only one who cannot stand all of this. She knows that. For here is Nana Amna singing now in the kitchen, her anger evaporated. And her mother, arranging flowers to perfection despite the press of time, and now her father arrives, assured and confident, as he brings a foreign delegation to his home for an authentic Egyptian lunch: a basin of stuffed grape leaves, rice with raisins and pine nuts flavored with nutmeg and cinnamon, and a juicy small turkey straight from the oven, with roasted onions. But before all of *that* appears, there will be a generously-sized fish served with mayonnaise and decked out to look like it is still a real, live fish with a black olive in each eye socket and in place of its mouth a length of carrot curved into a thick blank smile. There must have been meat and green vegetables as well, and then after all of this, strawberries sprinkled with rose water and powdered sugar, and mint tea—round after round of tiny, almost thimble-sized cups, that Mahmoud the *sufragi* offered around, costumed in his appealing white *gallabiya*, his head wrapped in a Nubian turban. There would not have been any wine, only fresh pomegranate juice.

These people who have come home with her father speak very quickly and devour their food, and make plans for the afternoon, and then maybe even through tomorrow or the day after, all very rapidly. These people are shooting flames of eager energy.

When she follows her mother into the bathroom to wash her hands she sees her mother drying her hands on a dazzlingly white towel with the same keen energy that ruled the meal. From her mother wafts the scent of oranges even though there were no oranges at lunch. She opens her mouth in a question but immediately shuts it in abrupt understanding, as if someone has suddenly whispered in her ear: There are secrets to fragrances and scents.

Why aren't the things that *they* somehow hold in check under her control as well? Do *they* suffer from all that wells up inside them, as she does? She flees to her room and snatches the rope that she can see half-coiled on top of the toy chest and starts to jump. That should release the bottled-up feeling that is consuming her. Then Amna comes in and scolds her.

"Your father's asleep. Besides, jumping rope in the house brings bad luck. Don't you have any *hoomwoork*?"

Don't you have anything but botherations, Amna? No sooner are the words on the edge of her tongue than the half-hidden feelings of guilt surge back into her consciousness.

Her mother always said that Amna was dim—even though Amna was vigorous, never seemed to tire, and was always clean and neat. Her mother also would declare that Amna was as stubborn as a mule. That made her wince, because she loved Amna in spite of the woman's hard discipline and wounding tongue. Whenever the grownups went out, Amna was the one who filled the world and kept it from crumbling. She'd sit cross-legged on the floor in the bedroom and tell stories.

"God forgive him, my father, then. He used to send folks after me to fetch me back when I was on my way to school. If I'd gotten education I would have been something else. *W'allahi*, I would have been something else indeed, madame—*ya Sitt* Kimi."

The memory solidifies, as it rises out of her voice's reverberation through the aching space that is me, while my heart presses the juice in my arteries until the red fluid spills into my head and I'm sorrowful as I think of her. I wish she had not called me "madame"; why did she have to choose *ya Sitt?* And anyway, something about that title doesn't sit comfortably with her words, or with the scowl on her face or the anger in her voice as she opened the door to me then, returning from my day at school. How can it be that Amna is entitled to change so mercurially, from a harsh tyrant who barks orders without mercy to this poor woman who sighs and mashes her lips together loudly over what life has brought her? She savors the lowliness, addressing me, a little girl, as *Sitt.* I like her better when she flings insults at me. She cursed me only in French, of which she had learned just enough to swear. You *parasseuse! Méchante! Imbécile!*

I hurry to console her. "Don't worry. Do you think it's such a hard thing? I'll teach you how to read and write."

She laughs. "*Yoooo!* As they say, 'Once he'd gone totally gray, they gave him a book one day!'"

She held a book in her hands. Greco-Roman myths. Neptune, god of the sea, stalwart while the ocean behind him rises in stallion-shaped waves, their manes racing, to curve and twist and break at the feet of the god. There is Diana, goddess of the hunt, spear in her grasp and sandals on her feet, their ties twining round her shins with delicate grace. Kimi is about to share the book with Amna; at the very last instant she draws back. Her hand has already pushed slightly forward, but she has kept herself from calling out, "Look!"

Most fortunately, Amna did not notice me, for she was busy getting to her feet—a warning in itself that bedtime was here. Even as she was leaving my room, pulling the door shut behind her, I was creeping from my bed, my body shaking off sleep with every beat of my heart. I was longing to capture something. Something in its very essence: the whole world, perhaps? Either the whole world or none of it.

I open my satchel and pull out my pencil case. I do a forbidden thing: I tear a page from the middle of my art notebook. If I were to take out a page from the back of the notebook, the other half of the leaf of paper would slide out from the front and Mrs. Fahmy would give me a tongue-lashing. The leaves of notebooks are a sacred trust. Only those lacking in self-respect and devoid of good upbringing would lay a hand on them. Only the likes of Lamyaa', who arrived at school in the mornings looking as if she had gone to sleep the night before in her school uniform, and having woken up in it, dashed to school, without even washing her face or combing her hair either. Precision, orderliness, tidiness, and cleanliness, and a sternly disciplined attitude toward oneself: all I had learned was strewn wide now by the magic of that large rectangle of pure white paper. I opened the notebook at its precise middle and saw the staples that denied each leaf of paper its own wholeness, dividing it in two, right and left, those heartless staples agleam in the middle. My heartbeat, already rapid, thudded even faster. Here I was, on the verge of committing an act of rebellion. Grievous act though it be, the lure of it was stronger, keener, and more vivid than the likely consequences. A solid danger of discovery loomed in the kitchen, in the foyer, in the sitting room: whoever it was could barge in at any moment without the slightest warning. Once discovered, you would be transformed immediately into a feral, untamable Lamyaa' in their eyes. In spite of my musings, as if not subject to my will, the pen began to move, leaving lines in its wake.

Yesterday's lesson on the atom and its nucleus.

"Now we are capable of smashing the atom," remarked my father. And added, "Credit goes to Einstein." He smiled and his mocking eyes gleamed. Then he hurled a surprise at me.

"A third of three is what?"

The three ovoid orbits on the page jump and change places. Under the nib of the pen, atom, nucleus, protons, and electrons are transformed into a little girl with narrow eyes and kinky hair braided sternly into skimpy twin plaits. Across her forehead might stretch a red kerchief, perhaps faded, sequins dancing along the edging. In an embroidered *gallabiya* she walks, barefooted, along the narrow irrigation canal. No sooner has she put a modest distance between herself and the house she has left than from out of the tall reeds spring two men, who seize her arms and drag her back, as she screams. "Leave me alone! Leave me, let me go to school!"

On the facing page is a picture of a girl wearing a loose, very short Greek tunic, her legs slender, bound in the ties of delicate sandals, her hair pulled back and piled on top of her head, leaving a wavy lock here and there to float round her dainty face. Her nose is well-defined and her lips full, drawn to exactitude. Diana, mistress of the hunt.

She closes the art notebook and rips the stolen page into shreds, stuffing the bits into a paper bag that had been tossed in the small waste basket beneath her desk. She returns to her bed but Amna's voice recaptures her and so recaptures me.

"I was trying to get away from them that day, and I fell smack into the canal. When my mama saw me she beat her fists against her chest and screamed at them. 'No one touches a hair on my daughter's head as long as I'm alive and breathing!' That's what she shouted, and, well, that was that. Later on, though, she said it too, she was as bad as they were: 'Forget it! All that school nonsense, just making trouble.' She died young, I was a little taller than you then, just . . . up to here, see? I swore I wouldn't do it for them, stay there at home all quiet the way they wanted. I got out of there, came to Cairo—and since that very day, here I am."

Abruptly she gives her body a shake. "Look here, now! *You've* got nothing to do, you get me sitting here next to you telling you stories, and the next thing you know—you'd keep sailing ships from leaving harbor, you would. I've got work to do."

But she doesn't leave me, even though I saw the door close behind her. She goes on talking. I can all but see her, almost as if she were before my eyes, even now; I can hear her narrative and the story. The tale of *al-malik al-atlasi*, King of the Atlas Mountains.

When she comes to the end, she chants, "That's all, that's it. I was there and came here on my own two feet, not even dinner did I stop to eat."

I don't remember seeing her eat, ever, except on very rare occasions. She ate as if she wasn't eating. She lived in our midst and I never knew when she used the bathroom or when she changed her clothes. By the time I woke up in the mornings she was already dressed for the day, and when I went to sleep at night she was still fully dressed. She always gave off the smell of soap and Cologne No. 555.

When I recall her now, it's as if she is dead.

I'm afraid. I'm afraid I killed her. If we write people, do they die?

But how can I be certain of it, of anything? How do we shape limits for ourselves—edges to our beings—that will let us know, at their merest recollection, that each of us can assume our own clearly etched self, an inside and an outside, knowable confines for the endurable—the possible—beyond which we cannot, need not, go? How can anyone endure to write, let alone live? I cannot endure life—there is so much of it, and all so painfully beautiful, and I have no edges, no borders to separate my aches from the pains of others. I am

Amna, and I am her tale, and I am the girl in the legend of the King of the Atlas Mountains. Like that girl, I too listened when my father asked me what I wanted when he was about to go on a trip. Like her, I was the one who would say, "Your good health and cheer! That you wrap your own turban, father dear! And come home as you always have done."

Lie. I am the one with want upon want. With that greedy long list he would always come back, the contents transformed into things in a sack! *Record albums and bathing suits, hair cremes, sheer stockings, and boots.* But somewhere in the space between my eyes and my mind, these items inscribed by my hand on a sheet of white paper appeared like that entirely recognizable greed, that insatiable thirst to grasp and hold something in essence, but something that could never truly be grasped or held. When the hopes inscribed in that list for the voyage materialized as objects cast around me in rich disarray, I would gaze at them in disappointment and feign the merriment and gratitude that I—delighted daughter—ought to have felt. I knew then that I was a deeply ungrateful being, a hypocrite who pretends affection and love and happiness and plenitude. A deceiving wretch!

"I am the King of the Atlas Mountains. It is he that I resemble, falling ill one day with an untreatable disease. No one proved able to cure me, not a single one among all the physicians of the realm. And as is the custom in tales, I was prescribed with a remedy exceedingly difficult to obtain. I would be healed only when there came to court a young girl pure of heart, a maiden of untainted soul and unpolluted tongue, a lass who never in her life had wished evil on anyone. Yet in their moments of weakness and greed, many showed this girl nothing but loathing. And if her father were to ask his daughters what they wanted from him upon his return from the next voyage, the eldest would say:

"I want a pestle that will be heard in Rome when I pound it far away in the Yemen."

The middle one would say:

"I want a mirror in which I can see the nape of my neck."

And the young maiden would say:

"I want your good health and cheer! And that you come home safe and sound, and wrap your own turban, father dear."

Everything that happened after that in the tale was frightening indeed. For after the King of the Atlas was cured by the girl (who had disguised herself by wearing men's clothes so that she would be given free rein to roam and cure kings), this monarch resolved to learn the true identity of that peculiar physician who had demanded from him no fee or recompense, but only that the King not attempt to discover his true identity, and made him promise and repeat:

"If some day you should encounter someone whom you decide immediately to kill, and if that someone says, as you lift your sword arm, 'By the life of the physician who treated you, don't raise your hand against me!' then step back and do not harm him." And so the King promised. But curiosity kept him sleepless at night—as curiosity by its nature may do. The King gained access to the house in which the physician was reported to be staying, at the very moment that the two elder sisters also managed to steal across its threshold, only to learn of the precise time that the King would appear, as they also learned that the King would not enter the house as ordinary folk do— by way of the door—but rather would appear there by means of the drainpipe. So they commenced to smash a considerable amount of glass, taking care to produce plenty of sharp edges. They filled the bathroom drainpipe with the broken glass. And so, when the King attempted his passage upward through the pipe, the shattered glass assailed his body. A single tiny sliver pierced his skin, to push forward and forward, like a diminutive watercourse carving out its own gully, with effort at first and then faster and faster, easier and easier, branching out and out and out until blood ran along every inch of his body."

Even so, the tale ended happily every time. Nor were there any monsters as in the Greek stories, nor people who shoved little children into hot ovens as in the tale of Hansel and Gretel. Nor did good little children find themselves surrounded by dangers in the form of evil adults, as in the tale of Snow White. But the King's attempted ascent through the pipe transformed every drain and pipe and bathtub and bathroom into a spot where specters and devils were bound to live, and made Amna's counsel on bathrooms sound and rational in the extreme, the very essence of common sense:

"Don't sing in the bath."

"Don't stare at your face in the mirror too much."

"Don't clean yourself with your right hand."

It didn't occur to me to ask her why. I never heard anyone oppose these warnings of hers, didn't catch my father out with the usual mocking smile on his face, didn't hear my mother laugh and exclaim, "Nonsense!" So as far as I knew, Amna's yarns and commands, her prohibitions and warnings, were to be filed in the same drawer where I put the incantation with which she ended the tale every time:

"That's all, that's it. I was there and came here on my own two feet, not even dinner did I stop to eat."

The First Time?

At ten o'clock in the evening, three doctors in their medical garb stand in a lavishly appointed hall, against a backdrop of black and white and dull red marble. Amidst the swirls of color and precisely at the center of the round hall stands a mahogany table on which sits a bust of Jonathan Swift.

One of the figures brought out a sheet of paper and a pen and asked me to sign my name in a box at the foot of the page. At the head of the page, in black letters printed in a serene and easy-to-read font, I read: St. Patrick's Hospital for Mental and Nervous Disorders. Although I had already accepted the pen, I held back from signing. Suddenly I remembered why. In a voice that sounded apologetic, embarrassed to be heard—and in English because somehow I knew that they didn't know any other languages—I said, "I don't know how to read and write."

They showed no sign of having heard me, so I repeated the sentence, enunciating my words more clearly. The man who had accompanied me to this place gave me a look and smiled, but his smile struck me as mocking, superior, arrogantly dismissive of the wretched daughters of the poor who have nothing to say about anything and whose families prevent them from attending school. The others shook their heads. One of them dragged a chair over from the furthest end of the hall and said with a sigh, "It looks like we have a long night ahead of us."

Something or other led me to sense that they did not believe me. That it would be up to me to find a persuasive justification for something that I could not even define. But since they did not ask any questions, I thought it best not to start a conversation. The three of them conferred for quite a long time, and apparently they agreed that the professor who had brought me to them was the one of them most able to convince me to sign the papers.

"Listen," he said, and called me by a name I recognized, though it lacked the ring of my own name in my ears.

"You are tired, exhausted, indeed, I think perhaps it has been days since you have slept. I am your professor, and if you do not have confidence in those men"—he gestured at the doctors who stood at a distance, watching us—"you can have trust in me, surely. I came because you asked me to—*you* contacted *me*, to tell me that all was not well with you."

I shook my head in denial but he hardly paused, finishing what he had to say as if he did not even notice that I was objecting to his words.

I am illiterate, I don't know how to read and write. I am here in this hospital because I discovered the truth, on my own—the truth that all of those people have been hiding from me this entire time. In the moment just before the noise takes over the world . . . before the desire to sleep vanishes and my yawns are replaced by an overwhelming fear of sleep. It is then that I surrender to fate: to the truth that begins as a simple little word, tapping softly at the walls of my being, until it captures and occupies the realm of all possible thought. By means of magic speech it gathers in all utterances and all the passages and stretches and spaces of Time. It filters out all flattery, all hypocrisy, all sham, until nothing remains but the pure essence of irrefutable truth. At such a moment, the mind is fully incandescent and life is at its most awesome and wonderful. Individual truths shine forth, one passing the torch to the next. Comprehension flashes and leaps like lightning, wonderfully at a moment when intellect and understanding had been arrested, and all words had fled. This is when the masks of falsehood drop, mask by mask. This is when truth prevails and its essence shows through. I wish I could scream full into their faces. Why, why do they not understand! The issue is simpler by far than to warrant all of this laborious complexity.

I fled from the house of the good man to whom I fled from the house of my father after my mother died. There, they had tried to teach me how to read and write, but I was dim and stupid and as stubborn as a mule, and I didn't learn a thing. But my father—who raised me among his daughters as if I were one of them—felt pity for me, as he knew this evident truth. He brought all of those people round to his view, one by one, men and women, so that they would conceal the truth from me and I would persist in my fantasy, my delusion that I could read.

But naturally he was not able to exercise his power over everyone when he was at such a distance as this, though he certainly did all that was in his grasp. This man whom I used to think so harsh, so stinging—did he not notice that my eyes were narrow and beady? And that my forehead was very small? Did he not see how very closely I resembled a monkey? Why did he wrong me so, when he knew that I was a thing incomplete, a lowly and flawed being on the ladder of evolution? But God is gracious. He revealed the truth to me so that I would not continue to be everyone's joke. Even the workers in the library knew and understood, so much so that they delegated one from among them to make jokes at my expense, when they imagined that I did not notice. This fellow would etch into his face the marks of mental disability, and walk like a hunchback, and make his eyes look almost like mine, the eyes of a monkey, squinting, cringing, his face ringed in the thick hair of dim-witted animal natures.

I did not despise him; I did not feel vindictive or resentful. After all, his harsh jesting made it possible for me to understand, finally. Before me the bitter truth shone clear, and it was up to me to swallow it. To accept it—the truth that had been hidden, with such very great care, and that remained hidden all this time! It did not occur to me that others would know, except on the train from Belfast to Dublin.

When I stepped down from the train, the world had taken on a new dimension. It had become pure and clear, sharp-edged and pointed and polished, as if to give me a fine crystal in which life's images spilled over and intensified. The voices had already gone quieter in my head; now they were utterly still. So it was that I heard a piercing, resounding scream, and my heart skipped, just as if someone had died. I laughed to myself, to reassure her, my self: It must be that Esperanza Wilde is giving birth to Oscar right now.

I walked in the direction of my lodging, across from the train station, and fished out my keys, ignoring the source of that invasive scream. The noise that had now subsided distilled a single, terrifying insight: that what I live is not the condition which other human beings live. That my senses and my comprehension of life are not those of anyone else, of anyone else but me. Something very alarming was beginning to weave itself together there in front of me, slowly, growing to giant proportions as it came ever nearer, a fearsome cold tidal wave edging toward me to swallow me completely to bring darkness over all to bring stillness.

Consider the moments of recurring birth that they call 'epiphanies,' bursting forth in brains burdened with a chemical flaw such that memory does not accumulate along the walls of the neural paths. If we were to attempt an analogy, we might imagine a fisherman whose hands bleed every time he lets the line slip through his fingers with its bait, to draw that line up again with a small catch: even after years of fishing, the flesh is raw and bleeding. Some tissues are so delicate and incapable of learning, for some reason, and they bleed every time as though it were the first time they had encountered a situation that provokes bleeding. Some tissues do not calcify, do not harden, just as some blood cannot clot.

My heart bleeds now as though I'm seeing Amna there before me clutching the newspaper, staring hard at it, her tears flowing in silence. My lesson in reckoning sums has branded me, disgraced me . . . *she weeps because you did not teach her*. The fissure splits into branches, more branches, bleeding, demanding revenge. I raise my hand to lift my pen, ready to bring it down on the white page. But the imploring voice of Amna interrupts me—"By the life of the doctor who treated you!"—and I stop cold, afraid. For her?

The memories of those delicate tissues are fragile. Or it might be memory of a different order, not sorted by motive. Or for a reason I cannot grasp, this memory grows paralyzed, and being is unable to take in anything but the moment's agony, into which it dissolves wholly, slyly managing every act, as it slips back, perhaps, to the state of a nursing infant whom someone abandoned, leaving it without refuge or support in a perilous forest. This is pain's memory: the agony of every human being. Memory of oneness with the whole, and of being: before I became me and you, you became you . . . memory of love and of love's other face—and nothing lies between them. Thus is compassion turned inside out, against itself; even the act of drawing a breath becomes an encompassing, unpredictable danger. How can I fathom what hangs upon it, what dire consequences will neglect or indolence harvest when it is too late? Beneath the heavy burden of doubt—of worry: What course should one take?!—when there is no guide or hint, and the soul blazes forth and fades, advances and retreats—afraid anything it does will lead to its own death or to the demise of another; certain only that it would go willingly and submissively into the embrace of darkness if only some good lay in doing so. If only it knew why it must perish, it would die. In another beginning, the spirit will see plainly that it does know, and, knowing, it will not falter before submission. Before writing.

Was she—was I—born thus? Was I *born* that girl who sat down with the esteemed professor after he had accompanied her coolly to the reception room of St. Patrick's Hospital? And if she was born thus, how was it that they did not notice? Or, I wonder, did they notice but held their tongues? Or was it that at home and among her family, in her own language, those symptoms were rationalized differently, explained away? When her cheeks reddened from an inner vigor that made her dizzy, and she couldn't stop laughing and fidgeting, and when her will was broken and she was mute for a month at a time? How did they explain the rush of her heartbeat—she was sure it must stop from the very force of its throbbing—and then the utter stillness, followed by violent and inexplicable reactions and doubt about the well-intentioned meanings of words, and doubt about every tone of voice, no matter what sort of goodness it was meant to convey. Words, words were the small evils of every day. And most evils are small.

I did not notice them as they crafted around me a large bell of thick glass. I did not notice, because they worked it in an amazing way: word by word, every word a little crystal, skillfully and cleverly polished, with a chime and a sharp, metallic musicality. And from that verbal operation there flew shards that scattered and pricked my skin. What did they find so painful in me that they needed to isolate me in that way? Why did they so easily enjoy an effortless mutual understanding, so easily chatting the nights away, exchanging laughter, when I did not? And why did I feel this powerful estrangement, among my own folk— when my own folk consisted of everyone I knew? Did I, in the space of three days, kill them all? I wrote them, and I tore them to shreds as their breathing filled the room. For when I tried to take a breath, I found that their breathing had left no space for mine, even there, in that place.

The old red car turned off into the gravel drive, veering and twisting toward its arrival at the imposing portal of the hospital.

Fear, awe, his acceptance, his recognition through the medium of her writing: all were folded into her ambiguous, difficult feelings toward him. He was the only one she could depend on in such a predicament—that much she knew. Her executioner he was, who pretended not to have heard her wish him good morning or good afternoon in the front quadrangle or the dining hall. This obliviousness hurt her; she could not locate a reasonable explanation for it. After all, professors were meant to concern themselves with the students. She did not know that they were not supposed to concern themselves with students who happened to be women. In spite of this—or perhaps because of it—he was the only one to have won her confidence at that juncture; he stood out from many who had been friendly.

"Amna is very tired, Professor."

"Who is *Anna*?"

"You know who she is! She is very tired, and she believes that she needs help."

"Ah, I understand."

In a matter of minutes he was standing in front of the door to her room. Taking her by the hand, he led her down to his car, illegally parked in front of the house. He brought her to this place.

At the very instant I signed my name in the space at the bottom of the page, the feeling came over me that I had done something so oppressive that only a murderer would understand it. Who have I killed? What was I doing, the whole of three days, after the tidal wave swallowed me? It dawned on me that the voices had gone quiet. And then the notion materialized plainly, unambiguously, exerting the gravitational pull of a thousand black holes: if I were to write them they would die, and if I were not to write them I would be condemned to death. And there is no rescinding the ancient rules of the wise. A person who spoils the gifts of the wise surely walks the path to an irrevocable sentence of death. And since the wise do not themselves perform murder, you are the one who has to execute the ruling—you yourself, on yourself.

17 Westland Row

House Number 17 on Westland Row shares a wall with the row house in which the gay master of irony, Oscar Wilde, was born, sacrificial lamb to the Empire and equally its shadiest shadow. This building provides housing to fourteen women, all graduate students. Its inner courtyard gives onto a corridor from which a small door leads directly to the university's back gate. It's the shortest path to and from the laboratories and the library. At the end of the corridor, to the left, is a pub: Dublin is the city of pubs and clever talk.

On the first level above the ground floor is Room 14. Here there lived, for an entire and consecutive four years, an eccentric woman. One who didn't make overtures to anyone, nor did they to her. She imprisoned herself in her room, emerging only to answer a nightly telephone call—always precisely at eleven o'clock—from Beirut. On Mondays she received a bouquet of roses, first thing in the morning. Her mail was plentiful; not a day passed without a letter or two for her placed on the table in the entry hall.

Every two or three months she would vanish for a period that varied from a week to ten days. The rest of the time she could be found either in her room or in the library. She did not use the house's communal kitchen, nor did she come down to the common room to watch television. In the beginning they would try to start conversations with her, but with the passage of time they no longer bothered. Perhaps she appeared not to need any company. On Sundays she would wake up early and walk to Grafton Street to buy the newspapers, and then to Bewley's Café for breakfast and coffee. She was a cold, distant, self-protective woman, yet on occasion a bout of human warmth would overpower her aloof demeanor. She would bounce into the shared kitchen, engross herself in a television program, laugh to fill her lungs at Lenny Bennett, spin out a conversation with whomever was around at the time, cook, and toss off sardonic asides. And then, all of a sudden she would draw back as if she regretted having made any overtures toward friendship. For days afterward she avoided them all, stayed away, kept silent, and disappeared into her room. Sometimes she went to the pub; she didn't drink, but she smoked furiously. In the pub she held forth on Joyce, Yeats, and Dylan Thomas; and she made fun of herself: *The Kingdom of God* and *Exile* were written for me, she said, and laughed at a private joke that no one understood, and so no one laughed with her. At eleven o'clock the accustomed telephone call would come, and she would seem content as she closed the door to her room behind her.

Inside, for days on end the lamp hardly ever went out. She was writing. No one read what she wrote:

Parable of a Homeland

On the wall is a map of exile. On other walls she has seen such maps, but they were maps that conjured a nation. People who possessed such maps reconstructed 'nation' to their liking and hung it on their walls, recreating it across the surfaces of their interiors. She had seen them, in London, summoning Egypt 'through its objects': worked fabrics, woven rugs, papyrus, statuettes, photographs.

London was full of Egyptians. Here there was no one but herself—and the Africans. In the house opposite the station, the walls of those narrow rooms were hung with pictures of Geneva and Rome; one room was a diminutive Belgium. There were also little Denmarks, Chinas, and Germanies. Even Mary's room displayed pictures of England. Why did the map of her exile remain as remote as could be from her homeland?

On the wall James Joyce shoved his hands nervously inside the pockets of his loose trousers as he stood before a summer cabin, submerged in thought, his eyes blurred behind round lenses and a summer cap on his head, looking a little haughty as nearsighted people often unwittingly do. He is ignoring Samuel Beckett, whose incomparable head had been sculpt-ed from the expansive volume of Deirdre Blaire's massive biography.

Beneath them, Gauguin's brown girls smile to fiancés who never arrive, and next to the smiling brown girls is a cheap reproduction of a painting of a Chinese woman with a confused head, called *The Woman with the Confused Head*, looking steadily at a postcard that pictures an extremely complex directional sign carrying the names of no less than twenty villages simultaneously. This sign exists. There was also an old man with wide gray eyes staring in hopeless regret at the picture of a small harbor: a sailor whose face the salty breeze has tanned a heavy, impervious leathery brown readying a small wooden boat for departure. But the woman whose map that was didn't know so then.

It was a map that took different forms, to reflect affectionate yearning for a homeland of the imagination. No one could give witness to the existence of such a place, for it was a nation without territorial correlate, a homeland constantly remade according to need, its contours changing with the keenness of that longing. A longing for what? For the soul of a place that is beautiful and poor, a place where disquieted sorrow reigned. No one here knew of it; and no one particularly cared to know. Whenever she had found herself having to name it she'd been unnerved, silenced—if by chance someone asked. At such moments she had found herself obliged to *be it*. But how can anyone shoulder such a burden? Perhaps one can do it only by lying or spinning a yarn, or by clinging stubbornly to a certain image, or by purposely forgetting what brought one into exile, remaining in exile only to search for one's homeland, like many did.

When Miriam and Nick returned from Libya and indulged in unrestrained joking and sarcasm, what was it that they said to make her say: "Egypt is not Libya!" whereupon later she felt so guilty? Was it because indeed she had family roots in Carthage, and there were family members who took pride in their Bedouin origins? That's only one example. What she did not hear from her friends she often found in books and even filling the pages of newspapers. Tomes from the nineteenth century, for it was precisely in the nineteenth century that they told the truth and lied. How can any one person face all of this documentation of places that live in the heart, a living language and imagination, loved ones, and dates that are not in history books, or dates that one finds only in history books? How can one person narrate the story of a nation, and say, "My nation is not like any other nation," without falling into traps of falsehood and exaggeration? The original nation, the source and mother of them all, has seen its story ripped to shreds and distributed among foreigners, narratives strewn wide. The ties that bind it have been severed, and its parts awarded to the colleges of grand universities, dispersed in accordance with Dewey's decimal system into ten categories, in the way libraries are divided up and organized.

In a dream—or it might as well have been a dream—I stood reading the list, my heart all but stopping from the terror of what I had gleaned as the professor ended his lecture on Egypt. The professor was a specialist in history. And of all the pasts that exist, he specialized in the history of the Middle East. He stood beside an enormous screen onto which images were projected in sequence. With a pointer he indicated the photographs. When I glanced at the page on which my classmate was taking down the main points of the lecture, I was dumbfounded by the professor's astonishing ability to summarize:

—Ancient Egypt is a French invention of the eighteenth century, which was then stolen by the Germans and the English. They preserved its codes in the British Museum.

—The Empire of Alexander is natural heir to the Greek civilization of Athens which is mother of the European renaissance, as well as its father, sister, brother, and so forth . . . in Alexandria.

—The Roman Empire was a passing barbarian interlude, but it richly endowed medieval European Christian philosophy that gave us the gift of Gothic architecture. It was the cauldron in which the renaissance was smelted, of course, and it killed Egyptians by the thousands.

—The Islamic Empire: impossible to deny that it arose. It yielded artistry that did not recognize portrayals of the human form . . . and then, the Ottoman Empire, Sick Man of Europe, tyrant of Egypt . . . Napoleon's Egyptian Campaign and the Enlightenment . . . the Empire of Great Britain and the loss of India, on the road to Suez.

And where, among all of this, is Egypt? I reread the title of the lecture.

Yes, I had read it correctly the first time: the subject *was* the history of modern Egypt! Aah, Kimi, black soil, mother of nations: a story gleaned and narrated and sung only in echoes. They plundered you and became part of you. Have you now become part of them?

Between the passages and the arteries of her heart a civil war rages among all Egypts. And she *is* all of them: if she rings her eyes with kohl, so, and becomes Nefertiti; if she plants fenugreek and lentils in anticipation of Eastern Easter; if she recites Arabic poetry; if she longs for her father's house in Alexandria; if she recalls her mother's tales of the trousseau of her Turkish mother-in-law, and her father's derisive words about al-Azhar, the venerable Muslim university in Cairo, and its families of adherents. And then, amidst all of this, and from within these very images, she hears her mother's voice repeating to her the tale of Little Red Riding Hood on a sunny Sunday morning in the Fish Garden in Cairo, and Miss Cleaver reading Wordsworth out loud, and her parents taking her to Hyde Park and Madame Toussaud's deep in a Christmastime winter, or to the Place Vendôme at the height of a sticky, hot Parisian summer. And then at night she dreads possibly having to go to the bathroom where she might see the King of the Atlas Mountains as he comes up from the pipe. And if the questions come, she answers, "Egypt is the cradle of civilization."

And if anyone jokes as Nick did after his visit to Libya, she adds, "That's according to Breasted."

THE MIRROR

ndless days: she conversed with no one, and nobody spoke to
her. Until, one Saturday, she entered Green's Bookstore that
faced the college entrance and saw the poster, a reproduction
of Salvador Dali's painting *Metamorphosis of Narcissus*. She bought it.
Mary, who had the room next to the kitchen on the ground floor, was
with her as she hung it on the wall. She began justifying to Mary why
she had bought the poster, when suddenly she discovered that while
she had noticed the human form and the glassy lake and even the individual leaves on the trees, until that moment she had not noticed the
bloom itself: the narcissus flower. Her heart sank as if she had just discovered an annoying creature crawling along the wall. That was the
moment in which the beady streams of crystal flows that made up the
huge glass bell began to spread and creep. Until that moment the bell
had been protecting her: she had been capable of laughing now and
then, even when Tara had called her "Sylvia" or even, "Hey, Plath!"

Wake up! Get out from under this bell beneath which you are so
determined to huddle. Your end will be like hers. You'll stick your
head inside the oven, turn on the gas, and die a horrid death. And

because you have no husband to elegize you, no one will remember or mourn you. And because you are not a poet, no one will mention you ever again.

She laughed, sometimes even as the ringing in her head grew steadily louder: "Write me! You are the only one who can. You, only you, can pull me away. Tap, tap, tap. All of the music is in the timbre, and betrayal . . . and memory . . . ."

Tara did not know—no one knew—that I had a partner, and that he was a poet, and that he preferred Yeats to Ted Hughes. And whenever he sent me letters he embellished them with his sketches and called me Sheba, and signed his letters "Solomon." No one knew that I wrote poetry to him, but I never showed him my poems. When he came to visit me, the time before the last, he was getting ready to return to Beirut.

"You wouldn't recognize it," he said. "It's become a wasteland."

He was fifteen years older than I was, and I called him "Daddy" even though we did not have, never could have had, any children. It was not in our power to marry so that we might have children. The difference in age, religion, his status in a bigoted society, these things were extremely important for him. I accepted this, though I could have refused to accept:

"Say 'I' and repeat it! Say *ana*."

"How can I? You."

"Say 'I' . . . 'I'. *Ana . . . ana*."

"I seek refuge in God from egotism—You."

"You'll never succeed if you don't say 'I' at the top of your lungs."

"Just like *you*!?"

His eyes widened in true surprise and he fended off the accusation vigorously.

"No one can accuse me of egotism. I go to great lengths for others. Moreover, I don't complain. I do everything that's in my power for the sake of others, and you know it."

"Yes, I know it. I know. No. No—*I don't know*. I don't know anything! You think I am some kind of nincompoop? Why do you insist that I show you what I write before I show it to my professor?"

"I'm your professor."

"What about him?"

"We need his signature on the diploma when you finish your dissertation."

"Why do we always need things other than the truth?"

He is silent. He turns, leaves, and returns.

He had a wife who loved him intensely, and a daughter of whom I was fond. She hated me. Her antipathy towards me seemed to grow stronger with every meeting. I liked her because she didn't hide her possessiveness toward her father, or perhaps it was really toward her mother, who knows? I must have confused and upset her enormously. One time when I saw her in their London home, she was holding open the Sunday newspaper in front of her face as her tears rolled down her cheeks in silence. It hurt. My heart began to thump and that prickling, tingling sensation returned. *I am the cause of it all.* I shut out Amna, and I did not teach her to read and write. I fled from my father's house so that I could enjoy my life on my own. I fled so that I could play unattended, unwatched and without responsibilities. I rejected and denied, and I went on denying until the cock crowed thrice. I had powerful excuses, naturally, which became more powerful the more the noose tightened. He would travel, return, nourish himself on the fawning of others—he had no objections to anyone. He would go out drinking and return with the morning, staggering. He would come to me, his gifts wrapped in guilt—and I would accept them. He would force me to bind myself with promises that I would not go out unless it were to the university or the theater, and even then he wouldn't trust me. He called every night at eleven o'clock, and imprisoned me in long painstakingly written letters on which I'd wager my fading being and by which I punctuated the moments of a dead life.

He has become the only outlet and opportunity for any exchange with humanity. He has become humanity—and I've become a woman waiting for an illusion that condenses into a man twice a year.

I left Mary behind—or perhaps I threw her out, and she complied without question. I flung my coat around my shoulders, wound my white scarf around my neck, slammed the door behind me, and went to find him in his office. There he was, his hair long and deep black, assailed here and there by gleaming silver threads. The dark curls practically brushed the sky blue shirt collar rising from the neckline of a navy blue pullover. There he was: the eyeglasses, small, round lenses rimmed in thin gold wire; a mouth that reminded me of those O-shaped mouths on cherubs ranged around the murals of the Italian Renaissance. His brown eyes shone mischievously. We had met at a performance of modern Irish dance at the Abbey Theatre. As the others went on ahead, he said, "I know you very well. You are the woman I see in my dreams."

We laughed. I said I didn't like Jung's mystifications, and instantly he replied that he personally was Freudian to the bone, and we laughed even more. I hadn't laughed at all for quite a long time. When he asked, "When shall we meet?" that diaphanous veil of deception that separates two strangers fell between us. But then I recalled a young Arab girl called Maryam, opening the *Sunday Times* on a rainy weekend day in London. The newspaper had been wider than the span of her arms, and she had hidden her face in its folds and cried in silence. So I said, " Sunday. Let's meet on Sunday." And when the time came, I did not go.

When he saw me at midweek, he suppressed a little gleam of delight and swathed his voice in an agreeable, light tone:

"And whom shall I thank for this visit, three days late?"

"Salvador Dali," I said.

"No joking?"

"No joking."

"Do you want to tell me—when, how, and the rest?"

"I was hanging a poster, a print of the *Metamorphosis of Narcissus* and suddenly I recalled something you said that made me see."

I went to him in his chair in front of the window, which looked out over the courtyard, and I smelled the fragrance of soap drifting from the collar of his shirt. Through the window I saw the Henry Moore sculpture recently purchased by the university, a different perspective than I had seen it from before. On the soft grass, the figure submissively endured the group of schoolchildren who were popping brightly through and around the gaps between its gentle curves. I kissed him on the cheek and suddenly understood the distance that separates words from communion. You need very many words and even more pauses, and thousands of tiny motions, so slight that they are barely noticeable even to the trained eye; you need an even larger palette of tones, merely to signal misunderstanding; you have to pass through all of this before you reach a state where you know that your meaning and your words are one, no more and no less, and that they are instantaneously grasped by the person for whom they are meant. Before you achieve this, you need recourse to many lies:

In her room, on the small bed, she studied the long pale languid body. She had never liked white flesh: it had always seemed to hint of flabbiness, before this. And it had never happened that she'd known a man untouched by the purifying blade of circumcision. Yet, he left her synonymous with gentle radiance and rich fulfillment, his pleasure a slow, spontaneous, prayerful tenderness, a bodily reverence clothed in a soft tremble, a lesson in worship.

When the doorbell rang, he asked her, "Aren't you going to open the door?"

 39

"No.

"Do you know who is at the door?"

"Yes."

"Did you leave me knocking at the door, when you knew it was me?

"Yes," she said. She lied and knew then that she loved him dearly, unreservedly.

Quietly she pulled the door shut behind her. The sky was raining mud. She went into O'Neill's Pub and knocked back glass after glass of murky beer, and returned to her room, her clothes clinging to her body. She fell ill and raved deliriously with fever. The doctor arrived.

"Nothing to worry about. It'll all pass, you'll think it was a dream."

As soon as she recovered her strength, she returned to her hours in the library. But no matter what she tried to read, the words were unintelligible. When he arrived on his bicycle, shaking the rain off, he said, "Perhaps it would be better for you to go home. You have all the symptoms."

He was joking, or at least partly so. He knew that she had definite plans to go back. He knew she didn't mean it when she said that the only way she could possibly stay on was for them to get married. But she did not laugh when he mentioned "the symptoms," for it was his way of inviting her to his home, though what he always said was "your home." She surprised him with an anger that compressed her words and expelled them in a barely audible hiss:

"Where is my home? What is this that you call my home? Why do you say that—my home?"

I had a home. I had a home to which I would return, and a homeland.

It was not the newspaper for which her hand reached but Thomas Flanagan, noted authority on Irish literature, quoting *Henry V*. She read to him, a wan, tight smile on her lips: "My nation! What ish my nation? ish a villain, and a bastard, and a knave, and a rascal? What ish my nation? Who talks of my nation?"

He took her in his arms, trying to dispel her wild alarm. "I don't mean your *homeland*, princess of mine. I mean your *home*—where I am."

And when she stared at him as if he were a stranger whom she had just met for the very first time, he tried harder, differently, and got himself into a deeper fix:

"Where your family is."

"What's the difference?" she shot back, he took her in his arms and stayed until she had fallen asleep.

In the news, Egypt's pulse was quickening; Egypt stifled our breath. The Islamists: there were interminable lists of names, students and professors and officers and soldiers. They were hanged.

The BBC report wondered: Is Cairo calm or is it simply indifferent?

Cairo is a fish with mayonnaise, at an authentic Egyptian afternoon meal for a delegation of foreigners.

On Sunday he arrived on his bicycle. "All right, now I will accompany you to your nation, I mean, your home," he said, laughing.

41

She laughed, too. She was wearing black. She had been on the point of leaving for the Egyptian embassy to pay her respects, as exile dictated, following the recent death of the 'Believer President,' Muhammad Anwar al-Sadat, assassinated in the military reviewing stand by Islamists who had disguised themselves as soldiers, when the news came of her father's death. As she was leaving the room, her gaze met the eyes of the sailor in the picture on the wall-map, heading seaward in the little wooden boat.

THE ROUTE
TO SAINT PATRICK'S

I n the small room on the first floor of Number 17 Westland Row,
the light went out. The papers scattered across the room were col-
lected, filling one paper bag after another. These pages have been
carefully ripped to shreds. Here is the parable of a dream. What happened in that dream? And why did it begin with the Lord's Prayer,
and how did it end cut to shreds and stuffed into bags now hoisted
by Beth, the cleaning lady, who carried them to the trash bin? Scraps
stayed on in the corners of the brain: bits of a long epistle written
over the space of nearly a year. A sentence repeated over and over,
its fundamental meaning and basic theme comprising a single question: How can you be given to understand?

How can you be given to understand, when the only Sufi of your
acquaintance is a Pakistani who cannot say "baaa!" to a sheep, as the
children of that lesser god, who stand at the foot of the ladder, the deaf
and dumb, shout in the play? Did you see how the professor loved his
student, the young woman who was mute? Did you see how he taught
her to hear music? And so she heard the terrifying, hideous sound of
her own voice, the sound she released in her confusion and anger at

this mute fate? She is you; and she is me. No, she is better. She is in a better place than either you or me. He learned the silent language of the deaf, but in the end this was all he had to learn, in order to live with her, in her world. It is all in the play, of course. And after the show ended, if the speaking, hearing, actor were to fall in love with the deaf mute actress, how might their life possibly have been? What amount of daily sacrifice would he find himself compelled to make, to avoid hurting her feelings? How much of his life in a world of speech would he have to ignore or forget? And how much would doubts and suspicion play games with her mind whenever they visited others, whenever she could see him listening to their exchanges while she waited for him to translate the passages she missed while straining to lip-read? She who could only communicate with those who were more precious than silence, and more sensitive than silence.

You and I are like that. I live with you inside what I believe is all of you, and half of myself. And you live with me inside half of yourself, and what you think is all of me. We fashion a world for ourselves inside the ellipse created when two whole worlds converge, but we go on longing for the larger expanse, a space where people don't have to exert themselves to understand—or to misunderstand—each other. A place where they can have confidence in intuition, where they can react to others according to their own private maps. Where there is room only for toying with words, where no one can claim a blissful ignorance except within the narrowest of borders. Such maps are very private, very special. Such maps belong to people in their status as individuals, as *people*; they don't belong to geographical regions, or to the histories of peoples and the accumulations of abominations spelled out in official gazettes, over centuries.

Yet, how can you be given to understand? To truly understand, I mean; to understand within your very being. For geography, history, and the city, the metropolis, are all lined up in support behind you, and at the end of the day—and come what may—this, here, is your world. But it is not my world, or it is my world only by means of adoption, to the extent that it can adopt me. For it is not strange to me; I am the one who is strange, foreign to it. Any amount of arrogance, of disregard for those gestures, sometimes complimentary and sometimes discriminatory, clad in a curiosity that might be malicious or might be perfectly innocent, doesn't change the issue in the slightest. I still bear my blood, my faith, and all of these passports—Egyptian, Arab, Muslim—stamped by everything I imagine others to have been taught to imagine about that place I came from; through jokes and offhand comments and the caricatures in newspaper cartoons, and disbelief that it is not very different for all its differences. I go out to buy bread or milk from the grocer's carrying about the full load of that unfortunate heritage, acting as if I must dress for a *soirée,* must don my most precious jewelry for a bicycle jaunt in the countryside. I know well that the flaw lies in me. I know that it is up to me to strip myself of my identity, or to act as though I am nothing more than an individual without ties—that I have no family, no nation, no memory, and no longing for a place that was unquestionably my world. In my status as unattached individual, those jokes would not injure me, and no amount of teasing would touch me. The bigoted and the limited would not afflict me. Why should their words have any effect on me, anyway? No one forced me under threat of penance to come here, so why should I force anyone to bear the consequences of my feelings? But . . . Do you recall the Africans? My heart goes out to them. Whenever I catch sight of them in the quadrangle, I notice what you described once when one of the 'regulars' at O'Neill's asserted in drunken emphasis the weakness of Africans for whiskey. "Look," you said. "Everyone avoids them as if they had leprosy. No one as much as gives them the time of day around here except me."

Why, that day, did I feel that your love for me, as it flows from its pure pristine source, passes by a spot where a figure stops you to shake your hand, congratulating you on the breadth of your horizons and your exemplary tolerance?

I'm African, too. Why do I remain something illusory, fantastic, that is constantly under threat of being transformed into a continent in its entirety, or an ignorant nation, or a submissive people, or even a more ancient civilization? Why, when you can remain simply Robert Sullivan, whom I would introduce as "Professor of Logic and Psychology, who teaches Freud and Lacan an Trinity College." If anyone meeting you persisted in questioning me, I would add, "He's from the North." And if they remarked, trying to pin down the name to a sect, "Catholic?" I would counter defensively: "What difference should that make?"

Was it that sort of thing that drew out talk of differences? We Egyptians. "People in my country." I translate the poems of Salah Abd al-Sabbour for you, but the questions hover over our conversation and linger beyond its end. Who is that "we"? Precisely which "people" in that country? I am them, and I'm not them. I am that "we" and I'm also "I"—just "I."

Similar things, and leaves of paper, leaf after leaf: shredded in careful precision in the space of three days.

Leaves of paper that would not do. Lie. It is just that I did not know that they would do, or could be put to any good. "Look, you, under your correction." Leaves of paper that were written in English—that's all there is to it, and I was afraid that English was not fit either for telling the truth or for lying. For it is my language, and it is not my language. Is this why I so enjoyed Beckett, and Joyce? And Joyce more than Beckett? And, then, third in the queue, Eliot. "Our father whose art in exile . . . taught us to care and not to care, taught us to sit still."

Yes, I killed people, many of them, all of them. A person who ruins the gifts of the wise is like unto a man who has killed all people—and that person must submit to punishment. I silenced Amna, nine-year-old Amna, after I had given her a voice. I stifled and strangled her, and I killed little Maryam after I had seen her tears running down the *Sunday Times.* And before that, I cut Kimi into fourteen equivalent parts and threw her limbs into the waste bin. No wonder I was exhausted—it was a fitting enough response to be exhausted. But, rather than making a cowardly plea for help, it would have been more becoming to end my life. It might be that I ended my life by asking for help.

SAINT PATRICK

A second later the darkness lifted and I found myself in a long ward, lying in a metal-framed bed and covered by a lightweight woolen blanket. It was cold in the room, and I was shivering. Then a door opened at the far end of the ward and a warm light entered, ushering in the shadow of a woman in a nursing uniform. Closing the door behind her, she turned on a small lamp sitting on a desk at that end of the room. She seated herself carefully behind the desk and proceeded to write.

With the lamp on, I could now see a very thin woman dressed in a beige overshirt of coarse-weave cotton, or perhaps linen, long sleeved and tied in the back in several bows. Her gray-gold hair could almost have been a pure white if it had not been for the halo that the light had spun around it. She was pacing up and down the passage between the rows of beds, touching every bed as she passed. When she came along in front of me I heard her repeat a word that I could not pick up. I smelled a strange odor. The smell of old age, I thought at first; it was that decay around the mouth and ears that emanates from inside the head, a smell that afflicts old people who have not preserved their brains alert.

Later I realized that this smell was simply the odor of insanity. I would smell it hovering around Robin White, trying to attach itself to her beautiful creamy skin, but she was only thirty and was capable of warding the smell off. It was the odor of the mind's evanescence, the smell of rotting memory, fear, and humiliation. I made a firm decision to bathe three times every day, causing the nurses fits of panic, and Robin fits of laughter.

When I climbed out of bed I discovered that I was wearing a gown similar to the one I'd seen on the elderly woman. The prophecy was confirmed at last. I headed for the nurse behind the desk at the end of the room. She raised her eyes to me slowly, watchfully, with an irritation that gathered visibly around her mouth. I told her I was cold. She did not answer. She came round the desk and took me by the hand, leading me all the way to my bed. She put me in bed and tucked the lightweight woolen blanket around me. I shivered until I fell asleep.

In the morning I found myself in a room that held only two beds. Mine was next to the window, and to my left lay a woman with a child's pretty face, her luminous complexion velvet-cream pale under jet-black hair. Her eyes were a deep, fathomless shamrock green beneath lids red and swollen as if she had spent the night crying. She smiled at me, a tiny pink smile that showed perfect white gleaming teeth.

"I'm Robin White," she said sweetly.

It was December, and I thought she was joking, or raving. That year, uncharacteristically heavy snows had blanketed Dublin. My response was belligerent:

"And I'm Robin Redbreast."

She let out a short gasp, as if she actually believed me and condoned the name. When she took in the image of the deadpan seriousness that I put on in self-defense, she turned her back and said nothing the rest of the day. Later we would talk and talk.

The nurse came in carrying a large tray: a teapot, toast, butter and marmalade, a bowl of corn flakes, a large ceramic milk pitcher, and a sugar bowl holding fine sugar. She put the tray down on the high medicine cart next to Robin's bed and tugged at a part of the bed so that a wide tray supported by a metal arm came out. She patted the young woman's shoulder with a soft hand. "Your breakfast. Come now, be a good girl."

I was watching her closely. She smiled and said, "After your treatment."

I didn't answer. I had no desire for food, anyway. And I didn't ask her, "What treatment?"

THE PARABLE
OF NARCISSUS

Among the leaves of paper that were torn to shreds had been pages that held the story of a despairing love. Because it began in despair it was truly love, unadulterated by any of those concerns that squash love into the shapes of practical equations when people catch themselves thinking: Forever? It was a love that attached no strings.

On rainy days they would light a fire in his house in Dún Laoghaire on the sea, and then they would drink wine, listen to music, and gaze from behind the windowpanes at the sea as it frothed and churned. When desire burned they made love, long and slow . . . they made love as if they embraced deep in a cosmic womb that has not been yet named. These were days punctuated by perfect silences, for who needs words when encased in a profound understanding that eschews demands and expectations? But then there came a day in which Kimi's gaze out the window was shot with panic. In a flash he was beside her.

"What's the matter?"

She was staring at the wave crests, galloping stallions whose hooves struck the shore but could not reach the window, riding from the sea.

"My eyes are playing tricks on me."

"It happens," he said. "Don't let it scare you."

The thought that filled her head had begun to accumulate around words spoken in the previous couple of days. In the beginning the words, Arabic and English, nouns and names, exerted a mutual pull from mere echo and assonance, nothing more: waves . . . *amwag* . . . Maude . . . Gonne . . . departed. Then they distended, doubled back, collided, crashed, like ellipsis-tracings of atoms in orbit: wave *mooga* . . . mauve . . . violet . . . *moot* . . . death . . . until they ran, spilled, crystallized: Maude mode *moda* . . . *moot mooti* mine my death die death . . . she died for she had to die . . . sums, lessons, reckoning, arithmetic . . . lessons unlearned . . . Maude . . . Maude saying at dinner yesterday . . . "You think I'm just a pretty face!"

So Maude isn't very pretty, that's true. Maude is ugly. That's not the issue. Someone is ugly only if there's an ugliness within. Alternative meaning: she is very pretty but her inner beauty doesn't seep through to her features, and no one finds her attractive, that's what they say. It does not occur to me that she is mocking herself. Can't be. She's mocking me. She believes I fancy myself pretty.

Before the sea I summon Neptune to mind. Neptune, who filled the fancies of my childhood, and I wave to him, goodbye. Now I understand—of my own accord I told her all about Miss Diana, and I lied, I said that she was just a pretty face. I had to pay the bill instantly. What price, lying?

When he arrived from Beirut bearing flowers and gifts and I didn't open the door when I knew perfectly well it was him at the door—what excuse did I give him? What did I say, over lunch the next day? How many children have I made cry?!

When you move between two languages, your odds of stumbling upon word affinities increase twofold. Robert does not know Arabic. After two days of love and wine, Robert's lot was a woman dying of cold in his bed. She wouldn't talk to him; she did not want to tell him what was wrong. How could he not know what was wrong with her—he with whom she conversed at length through perfect silences, she who felt the heavy need for words only in the presence of strangers?

He brought her food in bed, and asked in the tones we reserve for those we know well. "Did Maude upset you?"

With her next breath, her heart beating violently, she assembled all of the nerve needed to discard the pith of self-pity that the thought of death had produced.

"No, no—Maude is lovely! She's unbelievably beautiful."

And then he laughs, and she knows—he thinks she is talking about herself . . . .

Deep inside her head, fissures appear: The crystal shard. She pats him on the shoulder and smiles consolingly. Not Maude. La mode.

Moda. What's fashionable. When my father was still making his trips abroad, Egypt was closed to the economic energies of the outside world. My friends had their dresses made by seamstresses who made house calls, but I wore what was *moda*, the latest fashion; and I wore it as soon as it appeared in London and Paris. I would stand before my mirror for hours, getting ready to go to the club on Fridays. I wasn't in love with anyone—and now, looking back, I am certain that no one could have possibly loved me. How can someone love *moda*? And I am an outdated *moda*. My head and I—we are *so* old-fashioned. I am no *moda*.

I like it when men take notice of me. I take interest in my clothes, I take care of my appearance, and I want you to love me despite my own strong-willed self. To insist on marrying me even though I shall refuse.

I'm just a pretty face

And so, next time the doorbell rings, I will not open the door to you. For then you would see what they did to my face when they took me "for treatment."

The doctors had been saying for some time that only electric shock treatment would work. My brother flew in specially to sign the necessary papers. I yielded my arm to the nurse who found a protruding vein in my right arm and inserted her anesthetic-filled needle. Before the drug took full effect, I heard Amna's voice close to my ear. "Don't look at your *nafs* in the mirror so much. A body who stares at its soul in the mirror is liable to go mad."

I could feel them opening my mouth and introducing a leather tongue. You hear that in cases like this, they tie down your legs and arms, and they fit a metal crown connected to an electric outlet around your skull. They press a button to release a calibrated voltage. They don't want to kill you before you can die on your own.

When I opened my eyes, my gaze met a metal frame painted white, filled in by long white curtains that hung in long starched folds, attached securely to the foot of the frame. I shifted my gaze to the right. There was the window. So I had not left the room? Or had I left it, but then they'd brought me back? And why this curtained screen? What were they doing with me? I put all my will into climbing out of bed, my insides boiling with anger and embarrassment: What were they doing to me? What was it that called for concealment behind a screen partition?

As I slid off the bed, I tottered and reeled and collided into the screen. My head all but exploded in pain. I counted my steps, feeling my way. I was very, very thirsty. A nurse came into the room at a run, as if she had known that I was getting out of bed, and before I could try to climb back in, her hand was guiding me gently and firmly, an utterly neutral expression on her face. She patted the blanket into place around me and left the room with the same efficient, unbroken precision of movement that had orchestrated her entrance.

The electric shocks were repeated. One day I heard them murmuring "lithium" and I looked at Robin, who was shaking her head. In a weak voice she said, "It makes your eyelids swell up, and you gain weight. It makes you feel like an old drunk," and she touched her perfect nose.

Had they given me lithium I would not have known the difference. The nurse always came in at the same times of day and in the middle of the night. She always carried a small translucent plastic cup and another cup filled with water. She would hold out her hand, with an innumerable number of pills in a variety of colors, and she did not leave until she was sure that I had swallowed them all, down to the very last one: the tiny pink pill.

IN MY FATHER'S HOUSE

The return journey is difficult and slow. So many minutiae attend a farewell. I gather my things. I stare at the wall some more, and then I go back to packing my bags. In the end I decide to leave nothing behind. I climb onto the bed and take down the poster, *The Metamorphosis of Narcissus*. Carefully, I roll it into a long tube, and by the time that Beth comes in to ask if I need help, I have finished sealing the edges of the poster with tape. I hoist the poster in its new shape and look through the tube.

"This is what they call tunnel vision." And we laugh at nothing in particular.

She accompanies me down the steps, with my suitcases, and helps me into the waiting taxi. On the way to the airport I feel the absolute fragility of my being. My body has grown so thin that it practically exposes the self within. If selves inhabited bodies rather than the other way round, then these passersby should be able to watch the images of two months gone by on the screen of the self that my body has become.

In the airport, I long to bathe. The odor of madness pursues me, an avid hunter, and there is nowhere to escape. The look in people's eyes confirms their awareness that I have just left a place that defines the border between those who are healthy and strong, and those whom the healthy and strong grudgingly endure. On the flight, I do not eat or sleep or smoke. When we arrive in Cairo and I carry my bags from the terminal, I feel the intense heat even though it is still January. The sun is very bright, and not a shadow is in sight. Nowhere do clouds interrupt the blueness of the sky. When at last the taxi arrives at our door, my heart quickens and I can feel it pounding all the way to my head. I console myself with a chimera, a willful hope unchallenged by my memory: no words echo from the past, no image is deposited across time. The mirrors of memory remain blank, neutral, the hue of mercury—mirrors in waiting. But I persist; stubbornly, I go on hoping. There, when I arrive at the house, they will understand. I leap the stairs into the building two at a time and pull open the elevator door with a shaking hand. I jab the button and when I reach the third floor my spirits sink, seeping into my feet as though seeking a way out. I arrive at the door to our apartment and ring the bell. I almost kick the door so they will hurry. When Amna opens it, she shows no surprise, no particular pleasure. She looks tired.

"Praise God upon your return, my dear."

I hug her but she slips out of my embrace, repelling any acknowledgement of belonging, though I'm not sure to what. Or, I wonder, has she smelled the odor of madness? What did they tell her? They must have said things. After all, she had not heard my voice on the telephone for nearly three months. In my head, I make excuses for her. I carry my bags into my old room and hear her say, wearily, "Your mother is out, paying her respects to some folks in mourning. Do you want to eat now or will you wait for her?"

I inspect her in silence. She has gained a bit of weight. So she does eat, after all. Heavy lines circle her eyes but her teeth are still strong and white. Her frown has become a permanent part of her face. Two long lines separate her sparse eyebrows. Our eyes meet and I avert mine. I am abashed before all of this harsh, strong, fearsome beauty, and so I'm silent. But she returns; we're brought together by the sitting room and my suitcases.

"Dinner?"

With my response I try to draw her into a space that was our possession, ours alone. "I was there and came back on my own two feet, not even dinner did I stop to eat."

"You still remember?"

"D'you think you're the only one who remembers everything?"

I can see her compress her lips. A tone of threatening sarcasm interleaves her voice.

"Okay, then, tell it—show me!"

"Later I'll tell you."

"Not then not now! Go on and wash your face, change your clothes, while I get you something to eat. Looks like your mother will be late."

After an absence of ten years I went into my room and put my bags down next to the window. I sat down, just to let myself breathe in this place. I counted the breaths that occupied my room while I was so distant, all the life that was spun while I was far away, the number of times the beds were made and meals were prepared, all of the conversations that I didn't hear, and all the little deceptions, all of the clothes bought and discarded and the number of times they were washed, the baskets of oranges squeezed, the accusations exchanged, the number of books read. All of the mementos—the breaths that crept into all of the places I had claimed as mine, crept sunrise after sunrise; and every time another day vanished, those breaths grew and multiplied and pushed out my belongings and occupied the spaces I left behind. It all seemed as it should be: the rooms of those who leave are released to those who stay.

I opened my wardrobe and saw that it was crammed with clothes that weren't mine. I swept my gaze across the place, searching for things I had left here for my return, but I didn't find them. When I did find things, they had changed in the way that things do change when they're transferred from owner to owner.

The blue delft mug was empty now of pens and pencils. There was no longer any black Squibb ink next to the mug, and no paper. Now, next to the mug sat a matching vase that someone had given me on some occasion or other. My mother says that it is my sister's, and I believe her, because the voice in my head runs a commentary on the room's new look, remarks in time to the rhythm of my pulse: you let go, you let go, you abandoned it all. This is the punishment of those who abandon it all.

The books on the shelves are not those of earlier times, either, or the dolls; pictures and posters have been taken down from the walls. My room has a well-ordered appearance, now, harboring objects that are mine along with those that are not, as if the Hoover they used to clean the room has sucked out the spirit of my belongings as it sucked up the dirt. The things I owned have died, although some of them still lie here, embalmed corpses. Had I returned instead to find my things moth-eaten, and the corners of the room giving off the odor of many years' dust, I would have reclaimed it from neglect; and it would have come back to me, to welcome me back into my own space, the very same place I had left behind, with its own particular look. And those things of mine would have responded to my renewed presence. But I was not the one who replaced or moved them. I was only the one who betrayed them. I made them serve me as a ready refuge, so that when life harassed me I could resort to my imagined sanctuary. I could arrange it as I wished, or wrap myself in memories of those objects huddling there on a shelf in a faraway room. They fulfilled the objective: ultimate consolation, the consolation of death. If I had told my story, my story of these things, perhaps I would not have suffered this sickness of the spirit. But the things we merely describe, without telling their story, repeat themselves, each time—in the museum, in the sitting room, in the figure of a woman waiting for a call every day at eleven in the evening. They're always there.

They don't move, don't leave, don't change. Each one is an embalmed corpse: it has not revealed a story.

It didn't occur to me that, if I returned to my father's home, I'd be made to pretend that I had never left it. That I would be forced to put myself in the path of a mental Hoover that would suck in my spirit with the dust of sorrow and pain, preserving my outward form and aspect while swallowing my story. This was not asked of me. No one breathed a word. But something in the very air of the place said it. "Here we accept only a single tale—and this, only if a tale must be told":

"Once upon a time, in days present, there lived a maiden of intelligence, quick and clean and innocent, sometimes to the point of naïveté. She read many books but we absolved her from all temptation and all tests, and we did not permit her to feel pain. We gave her amply of all life's byways, indeed, we left her in luxury. And when she wanted to complete her education, we sent her to a highly respected university in a conservative Catholic country. We kept careful watch over her, supervising her exemplary behavior by way of an admirable Arab professor who took it upon himself to select her area of study in a university where he was regularly in attendance. He personally read all that she wrote, and directed and counseled and protected her. This maiden was obedient, persistent, hardworking, and chaste. Never a day did she annoy or trouble anyone. She would go to the library; she would come home to read. And in the appointed span of time she finished her studies and came back, and now we are most proud of her and we anticipate for her a fine future."

Thus I began to eat regularly and to sleep soundly. For this was all that was asked of me. Only this: no free reminiscence, no spontaneity of expression in conversation. This alone. No healing tale. For no one asked. No one showed the slightest hint of curiosity. What happened; how did it happen; how was it that you felt no danger? Why did your letters not betray that anything was amiss? How did you conceal the pain from your voice when we spoke to you on the telephone? No one asked. So I gave no answers. It became imperative to pretend. Pretense in one place, and in the other. Appearances, here just like there.

I gaze at the wall that rises above my bed and I can see the other one, its rival in Dublin. That one is blank too. Walls without maps, here and there. And I am no longer here, nor there. I stand in a purgatory from which no exit can be hoped, not even in one's imagination. 'Limbo' is a more accurate word for that space which is made when two worlds intersect and partly merge. The elliptical space, the wheel of fortune, that threatens to squeeze the human shape standing inside, its legs and arms spread wide, stretched to the limit to resist, to push outward with all its given strength so as not to fit inside those two circles, for then they can annihilate it. How can you be made to understand? How can you, when you have imposed the notion that everything is perfectly fine with the muteness that pretence must maintain?

The map of exile fixed to the wall was not a yearning for the homeland. There was no exile. All there was, in that place, was another homeland, another nation. A nation inhabited by its own images, its own brands of hypocrisy, its own deliberate silences and its own pretense, that it alone existed and that anything east of London or west of Boston had no real place in the calculations of geography. These were unknown reaches, better left unknown. The only condition was silence and the pretense that here was all there was.

The opportunity to choose became absolute. Choose! All things are possible now, so choose whom to be.

This was the hardest ruling of all. I had never had any training; I had never practiced for this. No one had taught me. I had never sat for an examination that demanded the likes of this. In fact, from the outset I had never faced an examination. My driver's license? They brought it to me, delivered it straight to the house. My identity card? Same thing. And the passport I carried, too. All that was required of me, under all circumstances, was a continual self-vigilance, a readiness for the reckoning. For I had to incessantly consider the account I would give of myself, even when there had been nothing to account for. What does the mind do under such circumstances? Consume itself? Nourish itself on its living cells? Review the available opportunities for a reckoning. Count the breaths taken, and permit the beast to grow inside of it, and imagine that the beast that feeds on it is its friend and guard; imagine that the beast is its own conscience, the compass of its heart and soul. Believing so, the horizon narrows:

You spoke, you commented, you looked, you laughed out loud—louder than is appropriate. You were too relaxed, too familiar, around people with whom you should have kept a distance. You sat without pressing your thighs together. You ate wolfishly. You gave your opinion on matters that were not yours to decide. You spoke out of turn. You removed yourself from others. You isolated yourself. You said nothing.

During the trial, the eyes of the beast are transformed into deep, clear mirrors in which a person sees herself as others do; the others become that person's conscience, and the mind records what it imagines others' imaginings to be: She's a liar. A counterfeit. She's nothing but an arrogant pretender! She lives inside fancies spun by her own imagination. She looks down on people; she is conceited. All of this the mind records, and the beast attacks the heart and consumes it.

In the trial I am asked: Which color do you prefer? Red? Or black? I don't answer. If I were to answer I would say: I don't know. They wrap their tones of voice in a stole of levity and indifference, but the subject they are broaching has implications that are extremely dangerous—and they know it. They want to trick me. I know that red is the color of the harlot of Babylon, the hue of hot blood, of the body's desire. The preferred color of lascivious women who wear glossy satin. The color of sex without love.

Black stands for death and dread. Black is a severe, uncompromising Sa'idi, a stern puritan from the south of Egypt. Black disregards emotions; it's the color of impassive punishment. It is the conclusive definition, it is disavowal, the color of non-being—the hue of heresy and apostasy.

How do you choose? How do you respond when they've stripped you of the scarab of the heart, your heart's protection from the beast of your trial? The scarab that was a symbol of life has been willfully robbed of its turquoise color and transformed into an embalmed, preserved insect mentioned only with the invocation of death. The turquoise is gone, and so are the gold and white and brick red and lapis blue. Of all colors only bright red and black remain. Hell and death: scorched faces and the flames of torment. How do you choose when all mercy has been stifled in the judges' hearts? How do you choose when you are stretched to the limit in a cramped space, resisting the pressure of two worlds upon your existence? Yet I resist until that last spark of consciousness, where wakeful dreams replace resistant sleep to intimate another life that no one comprehends.

Choose—either you, or them!

Choose—will it be your life or theirs?

I choose to die—to die, me—for it's more bearable this way.

My death, my death, *ya ana*. Die . . . me. I. Stubborn, clinging on, ingrate, and for so long! She-devil, presumptious she-devil. Do you really believe that you're naturally endowed to choose? My death, *ya ana*.

I swallow the tiny rose-colored pill and sleep overcomes me. So I check to make sure that they are all well, and then I let myself fear the unknown. I'm not really resisting death—it's just that I fear the unknown. It's that moment of submission to the unknown. The moment of giving myself up is the only fear I have. All else is unimportant. Just before the darkness swallows me, I give them my blessing. I bless them for they know what they do. Strong they are, and vigorous, and they kill with silence. Silence is sharper and more painful. Silence is the mien of the judges, of the wise.

Silence works for you and silence counts against you. If I talked, they looked at each other, knowingly. If I refrained from talking, they looked at each other, knowingly.

Now, I eat regularly. I sleep regularly, and I talk to no one.

Tell me: What is the difference between someone telling you a story and someone describing to you how someone told a story?

The difference is like that between a narrator who tells the story of the idol, and the idol itself. The fetish. I am the fetish. I am the blue delft mug that has been emptied of every trace of those sips of writing, the mug with the bone-dry inkwell and the space where there is no longer any paper. There is no longer any object in my possession. Anything. Thing. I myself have become a thing.

A shiny thing of stone fully and wonderfully cared for. Look: two eyes, a nose, a chin, and a mouth, two ears; a pair of eyebrows, lashes, and hair. No one looks into my eyes for very long, so as not to see his own image in the mirror of those eyes. A thing, nothing more. Without voice, without story, indeed without language. A body that hears and sees only. Under the stony touch is a brain through which the neurons' sparks fly, never growing quiet. It's a minute atomic factory that generates a frightful energy but since all of that motion is invisible it makes no impress on the features of the still stone head, sentenced to muteness after a lesson in reckoning.

How do you resist your fate through writing if writing is your fate? I clutch my pen. Before me, the white page takes on the blurred outlines of a phantom. I see small black letters in a highly ornate font: Hospital for Mental and Nervous Disorders. Even if I knew how to write, my language would be unreadable: all languages are foreign, and the tongue of my people is suitable only for telling stories. All of my stories are foreign, or would be if I were able to tell them. Who would listen? Even if the tongue is set loose from stone. All stories have already been told. All that can be said has already been said. There is no longer any truth, except in silence. Who cares about a story like this one? Listen:

All homelands are mine and so I am without homeland or nation.

All languages are mine and so I have no language. An individual alone, without a group? A frail group screaming in the wilderness? Who would light a fire in Cairo's spring heat . . . who would buy ice at the North Pole . . . folks who do not read and write? Or rather those who inscribe their very bodies, space offered in pain for comprehension and empathy to thrive, and no one reads them. This is a map fit only for the mad:

Gray ocean, and the desert, rocks jutting out in the midst of green, fields of cotton, Sinn Fein, Fianna Gael, parties for Nasserists and Socialists. Cead Mille Falte. Welcome, a thousand welcomes. The politicians' struggle, armed violence and poetry in the pubs, booze in the homes, Samuel Beckett Hall in the new Arts Building, Malone dies and Bloom lives, in Arabic, the river in the sky and the river in the Nile, coffee with cream and Irish whiskey in a tiny restaurant in Cairo, the beggars in front of Bewley's Café in Dublin. Poverty here and poverty there. Beth barely writes, and Amna barely writes her name; Dean Swift's Hospital, and Behman, the train ride to Dún Laoghaire and the train ride to Helwan and the rain. Clever talk. Fingers pointing, blood-stained:

"That weird woman who used to live here?"

"Black Riding Hood?"

"Schizophrenia?"

"The girl who lived here?"

"She got better," said Beth, the cleaning lady, with a pride that crept into her poor handwriting as if she was responsible for the health of everyone, "and went back home."

"Returned to her mum?"

I can almost see his face as she opens the door to him and lets him into the small room. I follow his roving glance across the walls, now completely bare. I hear his voice through her brief letter, the brevity of those who do not write except under the pressure of extreme necessity:

"And the narcissus? Did she take the poster, too? "

She didn't leave anything behind . . .

THE WILDERNESS

I stretched out on my bed, studying the wall. Suddenly the door to the room swung open furiously and Amna came in, that frown on her face, the old oval-shaped sewing box in her hands. With her entered the fragrance of white sheets toasted by the winter sun and tablecloths embroidered in gold thread.

The scents of talcum powder and cologne enter with her, too.

"What's wrong?" I ask.

"I too have something wrong?"

"What is it?"

"You don't know? Get up, go tell your mother that you're sorry."

Her loyalty was always firmly on the side of mothers.

"It's true what they say, only orphans know the worth of mothers."

"I didn't do anything to make her angry, Amna."

"So then why has she been crying since early morning? Will it be my father who made her cry?! Didn't you scream and scream at her as if you were deaf? Your voice reaching the end of the street?"

"As if I'm dumb Amna, not deaf."

"Deaf and dumb, it's all the same in the end."

She goes out and slams the door behind her, forgetting the sewing box, which stays on my desk, and she leaves the anger behind.

I open the sewing box and images pour from it. Pandora's box, from which all evils fly and spread. I see my mother, sitting in a corner of the balcony on one of those sunny winter mornings, dressed in a wool skirt and sweater. Nylon stockings sheathe her legs and she wears slippers on her feet, trimmed in soft white fake fur. She opens the oval sewing box and pulls out a pair of scissors.

She cuts out the minute shapes of things with perfect precision. I sit beside her on a matching chair watching her closely; when I speak to her she doesn't answer. Between us stands a partition of polished glass that allows you to see but keeps out all voices. I stay quiet, my eyes on the blades of her scissors. I watch.

The point at which one blade edge intersects the other requires something more than itself to attain its full identity: to make it cut. It needs paper, or a scrap of woven cloth. Just as crucial is the hand that will grip the scissors through those two holes to yield a new creation: a dress, a shirt, a paper doll, or even a pale, white heart. Without that hand, nothing happens.

Today in my father's house nothing happens. My eyes take in the scissor blades, one flung here, the other tossed there. The tiny screw that turned the sewing scissors into the jaws of a predatory fish is lost. When it fell out, no one replaced it. The lengths of cloth in my mother's wardrobe have lost their body, gone limp, bereft of the crispness of fresh cotton. And all the brightly colored paper meant for my amusement, to cut and paste, that seemed always to be wherever the sewing box was, has gone wavy, crinkly, and dry, like a rose faded and pressed between the leaves of a book. The white paper in my lower desk drawers has lost its challenge and its promise, bereft of its firmness. If I were to take scissors to it, it would not give off that crunchy, harsh sound—now that the starched material of fine writing paper has turned into limp, damp rags.

Something has stricken the spirit of things. Something vanished when that little screw dropped from the sewing scissors and no one replaced it. Things have grown apart, and the very weave of the air in this house has gone feeble since my father died and I returned to live in the wilderness. When time and place stand on parallel lines, never meeting, the coordinates of existence are refuted, and weariness doubles, to quash already flagging spirits. Life is no more than a series of lists; codes and blades lose their sharpness, and nothing happens.

Every day we wake up. Every day we eat. We bathe. We converse without gusto. We amuse ourselves with the images flowing before our eyes on the small screen. We listen to the world's news coming from a voice that sounds as if it, too, has lost a tiny screw; and so, when it attempts to bite the air into words, they still come out without substance, in emollient. Columns ranged in a line, they create no meaning. In the background, the images repeat themselves: *al-sayyid al-ra'is*, Mr. President; *al-sayyid al-ra'is al-sayyid al-ra'is* Mr. President Mr. President . . . and flowers in a long-necked crystal vase, two chairs, and a table. And nothing happens: in our house nothing happens, nor does it in the homes of others. It is as if all anyone understands of life anymore is how to repeat a semblance of its gestures, recalled from a fading memory. As though yesterday doesn't produce today; nor does today produce tomorrow. The place is vast, its history long, and its people too numerous. Equivalencies of time, correspondences of place, find completion in a third roster, and thus are straight lines composed: here is a scissor blade, and over there, too, here are leaves of paper, and there is the cloth. *Parallel parallel parallel*. The lists stretch from my mind to the world outside, all in balance yet there is no meaning to be found here, not in three languages.

Mug: naïve person, simple guy, easy to deceive because he relies only on memorization, on silent and willing repetitions. This is his distinctive talent. Someone who responds; aide, side-kick. Fresh approaches terrify him, changes scare him, and he concentrates all his energy on his ability to repeat a pattern.

Mousse au chocolat: a dessert made of chocolate, formless, ladled with a spoon. *Crème chantilly* completes it, as a further outrage, to induce nausea.

Nausea: The summer as slow as a dizzy fly. Utter emptiness. Graham Greene and the Quiet American on an Indian Island, imperialized outpost, fans whirring. It is nothing other than the smell of emptiness.

This list: Odious. All of the shirt's buttons are buttoned. His face is red, his hair reddish-blond. His body is raw, stripped of skin. Through the airport he lugs many belongings. Home from the Gulf on a holiday. His wife's eyes are dead from neglect.

Fitiwwa: A skinny, brown, sinuous youth, Egyptian, his eyes full of kindness, glossed in a light Gulf Arab accent—and he kills?

Our Father who art aware of no history but the biblical prophets'.

Documentation: In courts to handle real estate.

Newspapers, schools and universities, streets and commotion, garbage, and the odors of cooking. Buildings of baked unpainted brick. Doors in naked steel and buildings carved from green marble, with huge entryways and air-conditioned elevators. Scissor blade and a parallel scissor blade. The screw fell off; jaws dropped and straightened into parallels.

Parallel . . . parallel.

Bianchi Beach in Agami, a short distance from Alexandria. The wave-stallions crest in curly foam, lazy, creeping over the sand listlessly, to die before reaching the August beach. To the left is a dense forest of parasols, and to the right is a dense forest of parasols. The umbrellas on the right are worn and ugly, and under each and every one sits a man home from the Gulf on holiday, wearing a white undershirt that accentuates the thickness of his body hair protruding from under the armpits and across the chest. His bloated belly overflows faded swimming trunks, their colorlessness heightening by contrast the dense darkness of the hair on his legs as far as the upper thighs. He is bald, and the sun has not touched him with the hue of health and beauty. Beside him sits a woman nibbling *libb* seeds. She's draped in heavy fabric that covers her hair and surrounds her face tightly before it descends over her body: she is totally white. Her face is featureless, emotionless. The pair do not talk. They drink fizzy water and stare into emptiness. Every quarter of an hour, the man strips off his shirt, plunges into the sea, returns, towels himself off, and tugs on his undershirt. The woman gives off rivulets of sweat and does not budge from her low, small wooden beach chair.

On the left, the parasols are dazzling shades of color beneath which sit Coleman coolers just as bright. Blue, turquoise, blinding white. No one sits beneath them. Everyone is in the water or might as well be. From time to time the smell of sewers rises. When the smell assails the senses of the girl who has for the twentieth time rubbed Coppertone into her bronzed skin, around the contours of a very tiny bikini and the angles of visible ribs, she jumps up and reaches for a large bag, the color of the bikini. She takes out a length of fabric—it matches the bikini and the bag—and winds it round herself casually. She goes to the Coleman and fishes out an ice-cold can of Heineken that she sips as she stands motionless. From the bag she draws out a pair of comfortable white espadrilles into which she slowly pushes her feet. She waves to someone who stands talking to someone else on the shore, hoists the bag, and walks toward the chalets that line the back of the beach. When the recipient of her wave realizes that she is leaving , he stops his conversation momentarily and gestures to her that he will follow, making adjustments to his Reebok trunks.

To the right the children stand still, eyeing other children whose attention is drawn from their surroundings by bright-colored beach toys, held by the voice of the vendor plying his thin *firiska* biscuits, rising now and again, calling out the names of merchandise that no one buys.

I was still staring at the contents of the sewing box that Amna had left behind in my room when from a distance my mother's voice reached me.

"Kimi is a bit tired, Laila. You go ahead."

In a single leap I pounced on her. "Why are you so set on cancel-ing me out like this? Why don't you ask me if I want to go with them to the beach?"

"Because every time you go, you return tired out and for days all you do is stare at the ceiling."

I want to shout at her, but my tongue rebels against shaping the air into letters, and all that comes out is a long, resentful wail, and she cries.

THE CITY

You studied music and graduated with a degree in voice from the Conservatory, is that correct?" asks the television interviewer.

Without giving it any thought, the young man answers, "If God wills."

Times have changed. I have been away for ten years, and so of course things are different. If people have begun to say "If God wills" when they're talking about yesterday, then it must be that particular coordinates of time and place have met, and at the intersection, something has happened. Or else, how have people come to speak of the past in the grammar of the future? Surely nothing more was to happen?

My father's house is still my father's house. Nothing in it has changed. My room is my room, unchanged: the blue delft mug, lamp, television set, bookshelves, the two beds and the wardrobe. And the carpet . . . it was all possible up to a point and then it was not possible. There had to be a source of aid. Letters to Tara, Isabelle, Sarah:

Prayer?

Yes, I pray. You're convinced that I pray in order to fool myself with some false reassurance. You think that I pray instead of facing reality.

Instead of revolting. Getting angry. Doing something, no matter how stupid. Perhaps, for even my prayers . . . how can I describe my prayers to you? A solitary trivial thing. A weak, faint voice, that has no effect on anything and changes nothing, that provides no illusions (not even to me), that brings no benefit to anyone. It is the memory of prayer; the performance of movements in which I was trained in childhood, a pretense; it doesn't deceive me, for I know that faith is not regained through prayer. But I repeat it, clinging to the memory.

In those long-ago days I trained myself into marching the straight path without swerving. I practiced the straight and narrow path on the pavement as I returned from school, heart pounding, life *happening* then, with such force, with an audible impact—life with a pulse. Now an overpowering weary disgust with life often pursues me and I come to a halt. For entire days I don't leave my bed. I don't eat or sleep or bathe. I lie on my back for hours at a time, staring at the ceiling and calling to mind the slowness of Malone's death at the hands of Samuel Beckett. How it bored me, reading all of those men who described a life in which nothing happened. How completely the works of Sartre and Beckett put me to sleep, and Gide, too, and Joyce. How my aversion grew as I lived the life that they had described so well. Writing, I had believed, must be a celebration of the joy of life; the joy of life, I knew, was waiting around the next bend, and once it announced itself, humanity would dance in the streets, overjoyed at the ending of wars, poverty, and illness. I once thought that a prevailing mood of ennui and revulsion was something specific to Europe, which had grown senile, consumed its vigor, lost its ability to sing freely and innocently. I did not awake to the lesson even as I wrote.

That is, poets do not write of places and times but rather of where place and time meet in the soul. Poets write from the location of the tiny screw that transforms the two 'jawbones' of the scissors into a working jaw that creates meaning. And the joy of life is not the concern of poets. It's the concern of life.

There is no difference today between praying through poetry or praying by the Qur'an. For, if in the time of the Prophet poets were thought to be delusional, in our day the whole world has gone raving mad. How can you make out the difference, anyway? Reality is too harsh for the ear, too much for the eye. The noise, unabated, overwhelms you. No longer is that clatter in my head alone. These are not illusory voices calling me to kill myself so that the world may live on. The howling has enveloped the entire world. The howling has become the world, a true thundering that deafens all ears. Car horns and microphones and people wandering aimlessly through the streets. The colors are painfully dazzling and the voices piercing and everyone is on top of everyone else. The city has turned into a beast, and parasites of every sort nourish themselves on its bulk. Worms in the drinking water, chemical residues in the food, cement dust filling children's lungs, and everyone is screeching and the music clamors and pounds and the lights flash and shine. It's as though my moments of madness, the voices in my head, the clamor of my delusions, the panting of my terror and the whispers have grown and swallowed the world to become the world and hope is extinguished in a moment of complete silence for the sake of prayer: "like the long-legged" fly "upon the stream," the one that "moved upon silence."

Even this prayer, inviting the spirit to suffuse this deranged body, to assuage the sense of doom, to reassure, to return the world to its senses . . . even the magic of this prayer has been thwarted, for it must exert its voice amidst the screaming in the streets and the shrill cacophony of the microphones. It's merely another word, one among the many that signify lines that will never meet. There was a moment when I could imagine otherwise: it might be that the ancient prayer harbors a true power, a capacity to propel the magic of prayer into the soul. For iron can be filed down only by iron. The ancient prayer— faced with the alternative path, comforting, numbing repetition in response to that onerous tumult—blocks the noise. So, impatiently, longingly, I began to recite the Qur'an, as the accustomed peril surrounded and enclosed the moments, stung by the lashing of the microphones, threatening still more noise. My heart beat faster:

Lord, condemn us not if we forget or miss the mark, Lord lay not on us such a burden as Thou didst lay on those who came before us. Lord, impose not on us that which we have not the strength to bear, pardon us, absolve us, and have mercy on us, Thou, our Protector, and give us victory . . . over ourselves if we have been unjust to others.

Error. Error. I repeat the *sura*, twice over, panting:

"Give us victory," over ourselves if we have been unjust to others.

And the voice of the Guardian of Repetition mounts: You have erred. You have replaced the words of God with something else. This is a crime for which the punishment is clear and unequivocal. Intentions are not considered extenuating circumstances. Thus was the punishment sent down and the sentence became final. From that moment on: You shall doubt the very breaths you draw. You shall doubt your vision and your hearing. Even your heart will feel tentative, fragile. Never shall the white light be distinguished from the blackness for you. You shall remain thus, stumbling, never certain. Your every breath will be counted—either for you or against you—and only what is against you shall be reckoned. Your father's house is a memento of days past: it will not return. Your room in your father's house is but a momentary dwelling that you do not own, and it is yours only until your departure is arranged. Your city has become a thing not of this world, and your country—that which you called "my homeland, my nation"—is a desert stretch of poverty, and sometimes it is a timid, dark-skinned girl, a thing "to enter in peace," and safety. Sometimes, "its women are playthings and its men are slaves to whoever assumes authority."

Cover your face, woman. *Hurma*. Off-limits hag! Lower your voice, *awra*—shameful part, private part! A woman's voice is shameful, and is not to be heard in public! Avert your gaze! From what? From what shall I avert my eyes?

A voice sounds, emptying my head from all voices:

"From everything."

TALES

Tales are entwined in remedies: stories are always paths on the
search for a cure. A tale cannot be twice told even if it harbors
a nightmare. But those things we deprive of selves—things we
describe yet do not narrate—repeat themselves, to guarantee our sense
of security. They're right before us every time, there in the museum, in
the sitting room, never moving on, never departing us, never replaced
or exchanged: an embalmed corpse who has told no tales. What could
I suitably and allowably tell, when the fear of lying has made me a
ready morsel for those who seek their livelihood in telling lies? They
cleanse other's heads of the filth of memory when they themselves
know and do not bat an eye. Even now I'm afraid to remind them of
what they once deserved, and so they make me out to be a liar while
they go on believing: from the house to the library. Do not speak to
anyone. Do not leave with anyone. Do not exchange visits with anyone. Do not share anything. Do not write a single word until after you
have shown it to me. I am your professor, this other one is only so in
name. Every day the telephone rings at eleven o'clock in the evening.
Every Monday flowers arrive, spanning five thousand miles, all the

way to my door. And the letters. The letters surround and protect me from a danger whose essence I do not know. Why all of this precaution? And why did they appoint this particular supervisor for me?

Every few words, he stops and asks, "D'ye know?" His cheeks redden and his small eyes become even smaller. At first I always said, "Yes," and sometimes, "no." It was all meaningless. This "D'ye know?" was a refrain, the punctuation marks of his speech, and when I try to recall what he said I know that he said nothing. From another continent, another professor said, "Don't give anyone what you write until after I see it"; and entrapped me in affection and jealous protection, preventing me from speaking with anyone else. And a few steps away was another professor who said nothing, who extended no helping hand, and when I said "good morning" to him in the courtyard he never answered my greeting. Why didn't he? I would ask myself. And among my musings emerged the impress of those lessons so far back in childhood: "Professors do not *discuss* things. Acolytes do not speak first. Men are in charge of women. That's because women have half a brain for a whole body, and so their faith, too, is only half that of men. The image of my father saying, relating it from the Messenger, who was speaking of his young wife Aisha: "Take half your religion from this little doe-eyed girl." And he adds, with his usual bite, "So there you are, little donkey!"

And here and there, among the leaves of books, jut letters and words—cutting words, appalling words, words thrown back to me by eyes that shine from the warm gatherings of imagined friendships, denying, canceling, twisting meanings, teasing.

"What a life you Muslim women have! What a religion! Why, it makes you equal as are the teeth of a comb; one of you hardly knows the difference between yourself and your brother, prostrate before the Kaaba as one man."

"*Fascist. Nazi.* You remind us of how some people once behaved here—but we've rid ourselves of all of that! Look at yourselves. You remind us of our own past. Of our ugly image in the mirror. How can you possibly be given to understand? You did not live through the war in Europe. Your teeth did not chatter from cold and hunger. You did not lose loved ones in Auschwitz."

Why do people understand evil only in their mother's tongue? *Gory news from Qum and Tabriz . . . .*

"This 'passport' that you folks carry—why, it's soaked in blood!"

So I defend it. My passport is Arab, not Iranian.

"All of you over there hate Jews. Racists!"

My passport is Egyptian. I defend it. What is it that I am trying to defend? Whatever loyalties I have are judged suspicious in advance. What am I defending? My passport? My language? My faith? This is a religion, I say, that took from and built upon your religion. That's all there is to the matter.

In my language, even to mount such a defense is a heresy. In my memory, no one has uttered the likes of this. And I cannot create fictional personalities who could bear the weight of saying it. Every composition is an act of the imagination. And imagination is entirely a falsehood, a fiction—and I want nothing less than the truth, when the versions of this narrative are so many. In my language, versions are not narrated from the imagination; they are documented: This one is sound, that one is weak. And so forth. As for treatises, they are strongly correlated with the interests of the state, which are so encompassing that the state must watch everything very closely indeed.

"I have no religion," said Tara, returning Idries Shah's book on Sufism to my shelf. "Of course, you don't believe those myths, do you?" She gave me a dubious look.

After four pints of Guinness, her laugh sounded thin, tight. "I understand. All they did was to force me to get married in church. I turned my back on all of my faiths. Stripped myself of all anger, and let go of all I believed and trusted, so they would put a seal on my marriage papers, a seal of acknowledgement. So that my children would not grow up bastards. I love children."

We were talking about Trinity's society. About the Ireland of James Joyce, bigotry, and the arrogance of the Anglo-Irish—their class-ridden mentality and their attitudes toward those who are not Protestants.

"Yes, I know," I said.

And when Hisham came to Dublin I was happy in a way I had not felt here before. Now I had someone who understood that Islam was not fascism and that Brockelmann's scholarly works carried a severe and unnecessary bias, someone who didn't have to be told that Egypt was not Libya nor Teheran, and knew the context in which women were said to be lacking in mind and religion, and also knew how it was that the historical context vanished yet women were still lacking in mind and possessing half a faith.

"What exactly is it that brought you to Ireland, Hisham?"

"You, perhaps," he said in his usual tentative way.

"You'll stay?"

"We'll see"—and said no more.

He found work and a place to live; without fuss, he settled down or appeared as if he had done so. Often he dropped by after work and we would go to the cinema or theatre. We would stay together to read and talk sometimes through the night, and we knew that each of us was alone in a sense that even (or especially) this companionship could not counterweigh, despite its warmth, its occasional outbursts, its affection. It was a beautiful companionship, lovelier than it ought to have been, without quarrels or wounds. It was a relationship that encouraged you to go beyond customary behavior, while at the same time keeping you mindful of the boundaries. It didn't censure extremes, but it maintained vigilance. It made of the surveillant a palpable person, one with two eyes, a tongue, and a pair of ears, when for so long Vigilance had come in the form of specters whose hammerings might be faint or violently loud, but whatever their volume, there was never a face on those specters that one could confront. Never a companion whom you could love and fear, whose company you would fear to lose—the warmth of that caring in a world that did not care because it was yours only temporarily. A world that knew it was temporary, harshly so. Its friendships were temporary and so were its enmities. It was just like any other world except doubly so. The house witnesses a newcomer every day, and likewise a departure, and yet not a soul in this place shows either cheer or remorse at these comings and goings, except those whose homelands are beyond the pale of their budgets.

We had gone to the same school and our families were on friendly terms. When I plied him with questions, his responses offered glimmers of a guiding light when all other guidance seemed to have vanished from my path. And so I kept on asking.

"When the foreign vessel pilots at the Canal went on strike, what did your father do?"

Hisham would laugh. "He did what he always did—guided the ships through."

"In what language are ships guided?"

"The language of the sea," he said, with a faraway look.

"And Salah Jahin?"

At that, he returned to the moment. I had surprised him.

"The poet? What does Salah Jahin have to do with guiding ships through the Suez Canal?"

"I don't know. It's just that any kind of guidance has become like that—all non sequitur. I laughed at him then, trying to provoke him. I reminded him of the song:

Time's treachery, my heart, offers no assurance
And a day will come, my heart, when you'll need to find reliance
My heart trembled and asked, In what shall I have faith?
What can I believe when I've long been in disturbance?

He smiles silently.

"I'm just raving," I add. "Don't ask."

Here, no one comments if you laugh louder than is appropriate, or if you sit without worrying about keeping your knees together, or if you eat with obvious relish to the point of gluttony, or even if you drink until you can't stand up straight. Or if you make love without any love.

"Look," he said, "the entrepreneurs' culture reigns. Have you realized why they call you 'princess' at the university?"

"You're exaggerating. Anyway, I can't help being the way I am. If they had not stamped every cell in my body with a seal of propriety, spelling out what's proper and what's improper, I would choose the life of those you call 'entrepreneurs.'"

"You might."

"Not 'I might'—I definitely would. What crime have I committed, being a 'princess'? A sleeping princess? Born to sleep. I wake up to find death kissing me and so I go away with him, and afterward I sleep forever. What have I transgressed?"

"Respectability, a name everyone thinks is decent, a good mention to be passed on to your children."

"That's an exorbitant price to pay! That's a price higher than life itself. What you are saying is that I'm to empty myself of all that I really am, of my spirit and inner self, and stuff the shell with respectability. A rag doll sewn from cloth and stuffed with straw. Did your mother ever tell you the story of the good witch of the North and Dorothy's wondrous red shoes?"

At my words, his face changed, growing remote. But he did answer my question.

"I saw the film," he said.

"So did I."

Right then the rain began to pound on the windowpanes and one of us said, in English, "*There's no place like home.*"

FEAR

Hurriedly I stuff my things into my bag. Wallet, glasses, pocket mirror, and hairbrush. Amna stands staring at me as I snatch the key chain, and when our eyes meet, I give in to the silent command of hers. I go in search of my mother. I find her wiping the dust from the leaves of the plants in the sitting room, leaf by leaf, her hands encased in white gloves. She is muttering something under her breath. Resentment wells up inside of me, but I suppress it and smile: my mother is talking to the plants.

"Don't be late," she says.

And adds, "Don't drive after dark."

The house sits at the edge of the sea. Bianchi Beach in Agami. The sea lies only meters away, yet we cluster around the splendid turquoise swimming pool. My father used to bring us here when we were little. But "here" was a different place then, just a refuge from Alexandria's summertime crowds. We stayed in a chalet that was also just a few steps from the water. There was no swimming pool, of course, nor were there fancy royal date palms in the little patch of garden. The kitchen barely held two people. And now here's a mansion like those that vacationers find on the Italian Riviera. You can barely keep yourself from expecting to see a yellow Rolls Royce rolling up the white graveled drive that sweeps by the imposing front door.

When the cars rolled up, there were no Rolls Royces, but among them was a silver-blue BMW two-seater.

A light pattering of rain showers down, and the group gathered in a semicircle around the pool laughs. Perhaps it reminds us of times when rain pelted down in the school courtyard, delighting us as if we had been given an unexpected holiday, even though when the rain started coming down during recess they would shoo us in from the courtyard to finish our break in the classroom. A single school united us then. Now it's the memories that reunite us: of summers in Alexandria and Agami and the chalet of Monsieur Bianchi, the clubhouse at the Club Mediterranée where they hauled the water from the inlet in trucks, the Bedouin women who sold figs early in the mornings. And now—all of this sumptuousness, in the space of only ten years? Canapés topped with Russian caviar, a cheese tray that boasts Emmenthaler and Brie and Old Amsterdam, foie gras in the trademark ceramic pots from Fortnum & Mason, and glasses bubbling every hue. Champagne, Cassis, Mouton Cadet—and at this hour of the morning!

"May Allah never return us to those days!" said my classmate Laila, reaching for an offered glass of Campari and soda.

The others turn their gazes in my direction, measuring the impact of her words on me. The month was April, and if there was magic to the days it was black. "Happened just like this in France after the Terror," I remarked. "Then everything returned to normal."

One of the men seemed on the point of speaking, but Laila put her hand lightly on his thigh to silence him. He closed his mouth as the others exchanged knowing glances, and the conversation moved to the weather. The owner of the silvery BMW swooped as we were getting ready to go inside, escaping the shower that had begun to warn of true rain. At lunch he pulled out the chair next to me. We introduced ourselves.

"I'm a *fallah*! An Egyptian peasant from Copenhagen," he said in a voice loud enough for everyone to hear.

"And I'm a *Sa'idi*, a southern bumpkin from Dublin." Hearing me, everyone's curiosity was piqued. They may have allowed themselves some conjecture. They would not be disappointed.

Spring turns to fall and fall to spring; the year completes its cycle as always. He came to me with his questions, earnest, confused:

"Yesterday at the party—what made you deny that you speak English? You treated the fellow so poorly! Why do you toy with people like that? Why did you tell Khadiga that your mother's name is Amna? And when Muhammad showed you the health report he'd carried all the way from Switzerland, what made you laugh so hard? And just now, at lunch. Why did you say you could smell the sewers? When there wasn't any smell of sewers."

"Smells in my nose—I'm the only one who smells them."

That left him at a complete loss for words.

His steel-gray eyes stare at me, and I can see him swinging between a yearning to understand and the desire not to. Now he must choose. In the end he will side with himself. What impossible examination is this that I impose on my own loved ones? I insist on going out in public, appearing before *tout le monde* but in rags. I braid my hair without letting it dry first, and then I go to a formal function for VIPs. What's this? I clip my nails short and I don't paint them. I won't wear makeup, either. And then I'm absolutely determined that anyone who is fond of me must take my part, and must stand by me especially fervently when, here and there, a risible tone of voice can be heard. Even if my defender is the real target of the joke, even if the barbs lodge in his heart and not in mine. He is duty-bound to forget himself, to jump up in defense of me, of *me*, at any moment, always and at all costs. Moreover, with an alteration in the type of occasion, the party etiquette, the social rituals of it all, I transform myself accordingly. If the invitation states that females are not to wear makeup, that they must dress in tatters and put their hair up any old way, and cut off their fingernails and absolutely refrain from powdering their noses . . . then I go to that particular event dressed in the most striking and extravagant ensemble that I can find hanging in my closet, having made up my face with painstaking care. If my fingernails happen to be short at the time I stick on artificial nails. And I strike my pose, demanding from those who are fond of me that they show pride in me, whatever the cost to them, however painful the arrows of derision are.

For how can I possibly know that you love me, *me*, for my own sake and not for the sake of my jet-black hair?

Yet, I do try to explain. Yet, with every attempt, the opaqueness in his eyes deepens. I've seen the partiality indicator swinging away from me, creating a divide between us, so that we'll become two. And I know that he is taking his own side, against me. I work harder at my explanation:

"They're sacrificial offerings, to placate the beasts in the trial so that they'll stay away. If I could shake off all of those images of me, if I had no image left which would allow them to recognize me, then perhaps they would stop. If I could evade them, maybe they would tire of me or get confused, and then they might stop trying to hurt me. But how will it become possible for you to understand? To realize that these are my offerings, that they allow me to defend you? I pay my images, instead, I pay them as my sacrifice. False doors, doors that draw the thieves away from the gates of the true dwelling places of the soul."

"And what are those, Kimi?"

When he can hear no response, when he can see the tears welling up, transforming his face into a sea of evasive waves, he persists, driven by his own good heart.

"What are the beasts in the trial saying to you, Kimi?"

"They say I'm a liar. They say I live a deceiving, narcissistic life, and that if I don't destroy myself, you'll die. You."

"You know that's ridiculous! You're too smart to think such nonsense. Too sensible for such talk. Look at yourself. Look at the people who love you. Look at how proud I am of you—don't you see? Why are you letting your fancies destroy an agreeable life?"

"Lie. What agreeable life! I'll show you."

I walk over to the photograph album, that chest of small evils. As I open it, sharp word-fragments fly out. I point. A girl, posed in front of the Acropolis, smiles into the camera. Next, a woman holds her head high, chin tipped up in pleased self-importance, as the breeze riffles her hair in a stream away from her brow, for she stands on the deck of a boat at sea. Here's another one, all but splitting her jaw with a laugh brought on by something that is now lost forever. There's one, engrossed in speaking to a group of people who all listen intently. Shards of many other photographs, snapped in front of the leaning tower of Pisa, next to Rome's Trevi Fountain, on a Sunday morning in front of Buckingham Palace. A photo of Lake Leman seen from a window at the Beau Rivage in Geneva, another, taken in Amsterdam's old city center. And fields of daffodil. Fields of wild lying narcissus. There's a photograph of Amna gazing at the pictures in an old magazine, and one of a little blond girl from the Sa'id wearing a rose-pink embroidered dress, her blond hair wildly tousled, waving a dirt-covered palm at the camera, on her wrist a tattooed cross. And a picture of two tourists taking a picture of two tourists taking a picture . . . and Dublin in the rain.

"See? Do you understand now? All of this—what does it say to you? Let me hear that clever mind of yours speak! Tell me—what do the pictures say to you?"

"Memories, and of lovely moments, I'm sure. Times free of worries and responsibilities."

"Moments of Narcissus."

I reached for the photographs and ripped them to shreds, one by one, slowly, as he watched. There remained only the photograph of the girl waving to the camera with a dirty hand, and his last gift, a credit card.

Loathing erects a wall between us that blocks all tender memory. Our eyes drop deep inside each others', and I sense my head turning into stone.

They might have summoned a doctor. They might have stayed up nights, observing. They might have cried, and some might have consoled others. But what is certain is that I slept for a very long time and when I woke I was crying. I insisted on scrubbing my face clean of any cosmetic traces, though there was no makeup on it.

Next to the bed sat my mother. When I opened my eyes she smiled encouragingly.

"I'll bring you something to eat. You must eat now, and rest."

"I killed him, did you see? I killed him. If you had seen his eyes as I was ripping up the credit card, you would have known that I did not pay enough. I am an offering. When I don't pay with myself, someone dies. Every time."

Her voice is wise and even. Clear and simple in its use of words. "You did not kill anyone. Nothing happened. You're a bit tired, that's all there is to it."

"If I hadn't insisted on killing myself I wouldn't have killed anyone, you understand?"

"What crimes, Kimi? What killing? Why do you insist on destroying yourself like this?"

My mother's eyes are ringed in kohl. Her image vanishes, her presence is replaced by a robust fragrance of oranges. And now I remember.

I remember long days in which my head would abruptly, swiftly, fragment. My mind was not strong enough to stay with a single idea for longer than a second. It ran me from one thought to another, from one memory to another as quick as a flash and I could not concentrate no matter how hard I tried. I truly worked hard yet under the pressure of the moment's emotion, whatever it was, my memory always played tricks on me. Then my heart would pound inside my head, as my hands trembled and my breathing grew rapid. My spirit gave out, and I all but surrendered to that dark tunnel that alone loomed before me. But that was the instant in which they appeared, in all of their mercy. And they confirmed it for me. If you give yourself up to the punishment, you will die. If you do not, your loved ones will die.

In the end, I give in. I brush off all the accumulations of images and there remains of me only the shell, the penultimate layer of who I am.

DWELLINGS OF THE SOUL

I had an onion in my hand. It was the morning of Shamm al-Nasim. The ancient feast of spring. I was peeling the onion and when I finished peeling it I realized that the peel was all there was to the onion. I realized that they had deceived us, though they might have been well-intentioned. Perhaps they acted out of a stupid and stubborn adherence to false hopes. If only the lesson in sums and accounts had begun with peeling an onion and counting the layers of skin that composed it. If only they had told us.

"Children, you are like the onion. Your task in life is to be peeled. But because your nature is not that of onions, in your case the operation will require great violence and cause intense pain. Every layer of you is resilient and glossy, requiring a strong flame to strip it and to reveal the surface of the layer that follows it. In the end, nothing of you will remain. All that is required of you is that you pay constant attention. The earlier you can do so, the brighter, stronger, and more vigorous will be your existence in the layer in which you are living. You must endure the cauterizing flame that accompanies every removal of a layer, so that the new layer of your existence will appear beneath it. This is what we call Hell.

"As for the Straight Path, children, it comprises full attention and constant alertness. It takes the shape of intersecting circles. No, it is *not* a long line from which you fall either to the right or to the left. Paradise? That is the void. It is what all of us find in the end."

Would anything have been different if they had obliged themselves to tell us something of this sort? Would this have stripped from the world all that makes it worthy of being a world? Or would other tales and legends have taken the place of the stories we inherit here? I mean the particular tales that we are told here—for that story of the onion, in one form or another, is told to children elsewhere, children in distant places, who are born and grow up and die exactly as we do.

I wonder. Had they told me the story of the onion and its peel instead of the story of the Straight Path, which of those drills of mine would that little brain have then devised, and which would it have rejected? At the time would I have noticed that the paved walk leading to school really took the shape of a large circle that closed only in some intangible location inside of the self? That, closing there, it led to another huge circle, its rim untouched by the next circle, except at the single point where it led on to a higher level? That at the summit of this gradual ascent, the circle might really have taken the shape of an enormous spiral? And if I had been persuaded of some such notion, would this have meant a very different sort of training in watchfulness? Would that kind of knowledge at an early age have spared me the wracking pains in my head brought on by an unfortunate spinster whose sense of her own importance and superiority were fostered only by her skill at reckoning sums in a primary school? Would the story of the onion have spared me those feelings of guilt toward Amna and, later, toward little Maryam? And would words then not have had the power to wound me? Or were the wounds left by words inescapable? The excruciating pain that words leave is that fire burning the surface of the transparent layer of peel so that the next layer will be exposed. That pain is the clock hand—and alarm—that warns you when the moment comes for ascent to the next level in that colossal spiral. For the very same words, if said in differing circumstances, may have no impact at all.

There's a second factor at work, then, in calibrating the power of words to affect you at one time and not at another. A certain level of maturity—of ripeness—must grow from within the onion for the words to perform their task of shedding the peel that has grown hard and dry, so that the next layer can appear.

How did I resist this power for so long, to the point that I treated words as little crystal shards mounting and winding around me until they made me deaf? What caused all of that beautiful terrible harshness to lose its frightening beauty—and its power to create, as it weaves itself into a massive bell that protects me from change and blocks the natural law of growth to maturity? What happens when we insist on keeping those onions in the ground after they no longer need to be there? When we do not expose them at the appropriate moment to sunshine and air? Don't those onions spoil and rot? They become impossible to peel. They lose their own particular nature, the arc through existence for which they had a natural disposition. And we always give the same excuse: the right time has not yet come, or this particular onion, or the one over there, is too fragile to endure the sun's severity and the air's indifference.

When the voices began to sound inside my head, they were preceded by a tremendous headache that knotted itself vehemently inside of my brain as I stared at the onion in my hand, which had been peeled and peeled until nothing was left but a small twin almond-shaped kernel. I went on peeling it away from itself, though the job became more difficult as the onion's bulk shrank in my hand.

When I had finished my peeling, I stared at the layers of skin, those golden and silvery transparencies between my hands. In my head, the whole issue emerged in a few words. There are people. They are born and die and that's all there is to it. This is how things appear when the illusions are gone. Or when the reality of things is gone. What, after all, is the difference?

So! Is this the state in which people live? Is this my state when I'm overpowered by the other face of that fearful watchfulness for something to happen? And then when something does happen, I will not be fearful or watching for anything. For the sum of my knowledge of the world does not surpass the boundaries of my own skin— my own self-centered wrap at that precise moment. Had it been otherwise, I would have known that Hisham was dying on the tennis court. I would have sensed that, at the very time I was peeling the onion, they were going to his father to give him the news. Hisham's father was angry because Hisham was late for lunch:

"He can't come? Why? Has he died or something?"

And they answered him. "Yes."

From one completely unexpected moment to the next, Hisham was united with all of the people I've known who have died before their fortieth year. They committed suicide or they were killed when their fathers and mothers were still alive and blessed with steady income. No one seems to find anything in this that calls for astonishment. People continue to treat death as if it is just something that strikes people after they have been peeled down to nothing, when there is no longer any possibility that they will find a new layer and reemerge.

Hisham slips in among the ranks of young men and young women who did not fully pay back the debt of Hell. They were not peeled down to the last layer. He takes a space in my mind for himself and doesn't leave. Not because he died before his last layer was peeled away, but because he lived here and there, in spaces I appropriated for myself:

"Hish, don't you love Jean?"

"I don't know."

"But you don't let a day pass without seeing her."

"That might be so."

"Might be you love her?"

"Might be I'm addicted to her."

"She loves you."

"Women say that a lot."

"Or are you just afraid?"

"Yes. I'm afraid."

"And if you were to marry an Egyptian woman you wouldn't be afraid."

"And if I were to marry an Egyptian woman I wouldn't be afraid."

"Why not?"

"Things—they're always there and you can't avoid them. Her father and mother, her brothers and sisters, people."

"Would you be marrying them all?"

"Yes, I would be marrying them all and giving my brain a rest."

"And your wife's brain, Hish?"

"Most likely my wife won't have a brain."

"And you will continue to love Jean?"

"Jean. Or someone else."

"And you'd cheat on your wife?"

"I'm not married to cheat or not cheat on my wife! What's all this nonsense about, anyway?"

For three days they kept the news of Hisham's death from me. And in the instant that I was taking it in, the sharp sting of raw onion filled my nostrils. My tears flowed, my eyes stung, and my nose was blocked up. I found myself remembering the onion I'd peeled on that Shamm al-Nasim morning. Something is always left over. Something continues and never dies. Might that be . . . the smells?

The Last Time?

Days are either white or black. But days of drought are gray, bearing neither longing nor fear, without sympathy or love. Pale days, lived out under the reigns of mood-regulating medication. Gray days, killed off one by one at the hand of despair. Days that are bottom-less, fathomless, wrapped in the melancholy of a person who has come upon a mass of knowledge before its proper time arrives, and has no hope of changing anything. Despair without end, despair of mercy, accompanied by a profound deafness that wraps the skull tightly from the inside, between the skin and the bone. This is a deaf-ness that binds even the tongue—as if skin, bone and tongue belong to a head carved from stone. The predilection of apathy. The choice taken by orphans and little girls who never did hear their mothers say, "No one touches a hair on my daughter's head as long as I'm alive and breathing!"

Life is a succession of disparate scenes, and I am a spectator. Scenes beginning, coming to a close, and all the time my head is in another place. In spring and fall, and without this reassuring regu-larity, my head goes where it becomes completely indifferent, and it does not respond. It's all the same, anyway: to return, not to return. To regain sensibility or not. Matters, concerns, and things loose their moorings and their connections, and meanings vanish. The tiny screw that turned the scissors into a weapon—where words gathered and met, waiting for the codes to emerge between one sentence and the other—drops and is lost. Life's ironies and disjunctions collapse limply in a damp rot. Words lose the rough edge that combats the thin, worn sounds of repetition and spongy pliancy. Life grows senile and can no longer be revived. Newspapers, books, television, and radio programs are packed with elegies for poets who once filled their columns and pages, and the streets, with the clamor of their free, easy singing and laughter, creating meanings from the leaves of their hearts. Those poets, too, have been murdered or they've committed suicide, or slow cancers have consumed them. Those who remain are not reliable, for everyone has come to doubt the usefulness of speech.

The month of June brings me the memory of futility. The world is clad in the mourning garb that a hundred joys in our home and the houses of others do not possess the power to efface. "All the perfumes of Arabia" will nor erase the odor of that blood. They're lined up in front of their airplanes, the screens of memory behind them. They are on their way to the battle that is going to end all battles and we look forward to their return. We do not doubt their return. They might be wounded, and mourning the loss of comrades perhaps, but they themselves, our sons and loved ones, must return. When they do not return, we rid ourselves hastily of the smell of their bodies. The smells of gunpowder and blood, the smell of sweat in the long, long lines in front of government fixed-price stores, the smell of cooking oil bought at a subsidized price, and the smell of the cinema ticket with its added-on charge that we used to pay willingly: "For the war effort."

We turn on our televisions. Amna, in front of the screen, weeps silently. I know she is not crying over the fate of Masri, who was fighting his country's enemies. She's crying because when he paid with his life he was sacrificing himself for the son of the village headman. His death: a banal crime that can be repeated easily and meaninglessly anytime.

When I look at Amna's face, I know that she is remembering things I don't know, but like me she is mourning the futility of heroism. She cloaks her emotions in the tones of everyday, wipes her face clean of tears, using both hands.

"You poor dear boy!"

But I thought I was the only one who had died, there among them, after my head split the crystal of the dining table. I thought I was the only one who surrendered to the flows of crystal as they wove a massive bell that enclosed my existence so that words would not sting me. I thought that only I had become deaf, so that they spoke to me—when they did speak to me—as if I inhabited a real body but was not permitted to move, and someone—or many someones—went on forcing it to witness what was happening in the world around it. I turn sharply to Amna:

"Why are you crying?"

"Nothing, Kimi, I was just remembering my brother."

"So your brother died in the war, Amna?"

"Oh no, no, may God bless him with a long, long life!"

Just the two of us, Amna and I, the whole of the long summer months. The two of us and the television between us. And nothing happens.

In September, Channel One airs *The Wizard of Oz*, arousing an indefinable sorrow that had lain dormant in memory. Eyes grow soft and the tongue clears a path to the lungs and laughter. Judy Garland stands at the end of the yellow brick road, claps together the heels of her sparkling, ruby red shoes, closes her eyes tightly and says in true longing, *"There's no place like home, there's no place like home."*

Amna looks at me, smiling encouragingly. In my eyes she has spotted an alertness that has not been there for months. She leaves the sitting room and returns with a loaded tray. The smell of hot toast precedes her. The tray holds white cheese, olives, cucumber, butter, and marmalade, and a teapot.

I surprise her. "You don't like the film?"

"I've seen it a hundred times before."

"So why this time, exactly, did you get bored? You watch every film a hundred times and you never get tired of any of them."

She notices something on my face and comes over to the sofa where I'm sitting. She strokes my cheek.

"What's wrong, love? Just a minute ago you were laughing."

"I want to go home, Amna. I'm tired of this."

She invokes the names of God, and the power of God, and the aid of God in keeping Satan at bay. She places her hand on my head and begins to recite the Seven Verses of entreaty in such a low voice that the words are indistinguishable. When she finishes she pulls me to her ample chest and goes on patting my hair.

"You *are* at home, Kimi, this is your home, honey, and you're in your own family, your own folk, dear."

"Why do you smell like oranges?"

"I was squeezing oranges."

The smell of oranges overwhelms me. And I know that winter is near, and I remember the bustle and energy, the blinding white hand towels, and my mother. My mother—she is the smell of oranges. How did Amna take over that scent?

"You didn't use any cologne today, why?"

"I did, this morning, it must have flown away."

"Flown away? Flew where, Amna? Since when does cologne fly?"

She implores God's help again and pats me on the head. "Lord, was I to know—where was all of this hidden away for us?"

Now I frighten her. "It was hidden in the drainpipe, if you go into the bathroom right now you'll find him moaning in pain, and you're the cause of it all. Remember? You were the one who told them to put broken glass in the drains! You're the one who killed the King of the Atlas Mountains!" And now I laugh.

Right away she enters into it, so that she won't lose the opportunity to play—finally, after the interminable months of silence.

"The King of the Atlas Mountains is not dead!"

"He is, Amna. He *died*, now admit it, just once, admit that you used to make up the rest of the story to have a happy ending, but in the original story the king died."

She's abruptly mute and still; she doesn't even blink, and her face is suddenly expressionless. She becomes a mass of stone, and I'm scared. I've looked straight into her eyes. At times like this, whenever they lied I had to avoid looking them straight in the eye or else they would turn into stone. When I scream, begging her not to change like this, she has already turned away from me.

After a long sleep I wake up and the anger begins to take me over, body and soul. She is just like the rest of them: she does not understand. And, like them, she is all energy and motion. She has a strong spirit that wages its own fight for the sake of survival. Her voice is strong, her movements are powerful; it all comes from her faith—that whatever life turns out to be, it deserves to be lived. She's a liar like all the rest. As for me, I can't see any particular pretext for living. I do not want my existence to have any particular impact, and I have absolutely no desires except that I want this accident, my life, to go away and leave me alone.

Then the tears swell to water the stiff, shriveling spirit. A reclaimed sorrow leads it astray, to hover within the impossible. You can cross the threshold into the impossible, if you will just let go and allow what the engineers call 'entropy.' They say that every step, no matter how tentative, sends all the atoms of life into higher and higher thresholds of chaos.

After the soul is duly watered, the tears are replaced by determination and obstinacy. Now begins a voyage against time, in a pace twice as slow as the time that has elapsed. The time to catch up with. The thought almost paralyzes me. I resist, though, for a person cannot die like this, without obtaining some sort of meaning. If meaning is hard to come by in the best of situations, then what do we make of a person who begins life with everything already magnificently provided, for tomorrow and the day after and the day after that? . . . you have a house and family, and you always will, and you won't lack anything, just as you will not be required to expend any effort whatsoever. If it does occur to you to put out some effort, good and well— and an extra bonus. I know that much of the effort that people like me offer so earnestly will have no effect on anything and will change nothing, but still, I resist. It's within your power to bring some meaning. If you do not fear the loss of things, you learn to fear the loss of fear itself. This becomes the sole thought that moves me and it is contrary to everything they claim. If you do not fear people's opinion of you, fear. Fear. And if you die before you can kill, and if death has given you the loss of loved ones and friends suddenly, and it appears to you that you have made peace with death, fear now. Fear. This is your only hope, the only way to invite meaning.

DOUBT

oubt is the threshold of fear . . . is it not? It's possible to polish fear until it is refined into a chisel that you can use to sculpt and carve your existence. In fact, existence is doubt's best friend and companion; its highest fortress is death, and every fear antecedent to that is only a relative thing. Every analogy is measured by the decisive criterion. But what if death grows in the imagination to become something beyond the limits of the possible? And what if someone or other has the means to kill you and you die from a hemorrhage induced by mere words? Does that leave you a space large enough for the fear by which existence is sculpted? Every fear exists in the imagination and is fed by our conscious minds from memory, the repository for the historical features of a mercurial being that does not settle into a single state: me, us. Who is that 'me,' and who is that 'us'? If I were to go to that strange and wonderful cache where all moments of history are preserved in irrefutable images, who could convince me that the camera's eye and the photographer's hand did not intend a distortion here or an enhancement there? I go to the photograph albums and carefully page through them, hoping to find the answers. Of what was I afraid? Which pose did I adopt in perfect awareness that the camera would preserve it for me, mummified in a final and authoritative image? With which expressions did I compose my face? And then, when the camera passed me by, what was it capturing instead? And if I conclude this search with a result in hand, will I have arrived at the truth of this being that over time is constantly transformed, with every blink of an eye? How does anyone come to terms with the likes of this? How is it possible to say, "Things were *like this*, and I was precisely like *that*." All that scares me is the loss of fear, for only fear brought me meaning. Fear of words, and the loss of moments that were magical, despite *and* for all of the pain they caused.

The world is a narrow-necked glass bottle of doubt, and magic is of two kinds: white and black. White-magic days begin with a delicate, transparent grief and an overwhelming affection that envelops everything and is empathetic to every pain—though even 'empathy' is not quite strong enough to express it. The nearest that I can come is to say that on white-magic days, empathy is offered by a being so attuned to living with itself that this seems to exemplify existence itself. There's a great fear and a greater sympathy for that fleeting moment that does not last. Is this akin to the experience of those who claim to have understood the language of the birds and the beasts?

In the car, on the desert road to Alexandria, I turn the radio dial to the BBC station and hear them holding a mass for the soul of St. Francis of Assisi. Birds gather in the sky, forming a symphonic flock. Their leader gets them all to dance to the music flowing from the distant cathedral. It's a sight in perfect harmony with the moment and with my being in that moment: me, the birds and the sky, the road and the music coalesce into a single entity. When I arrive home I catch a glimpse of the portrait that a skilled artist drew of me. From a recess in the sitting room, I gaze at my face framed in that oil painting and I see myself wink at myself, and I smile.

On the black-magic days, the forces of ill have dominion over the world and all explanations are mere mockery, scornful of the ways of good magic, branding them as ignominious goals not befitting the credence or even the notice of intelligent people. If noticed, they must be explained away in terms appropriate to intelligent people.

"Purely the outcome of your own emotions," said the doctor when I described the birds to him, dancing to the music of the saint. The saint had another face, a coarse one, and he was uninterested in personal hygiene. As for the story of that portrait that smiles and winks . . . he began to laugh, clapping me on the shoulders in paternal fondness. "Were you reading *Sophie's World?*" Then he looked at his watch, a signal that the appointment was over.

On black days, clever interpretations are on the ascent. In their triumphant reign, they're backed up by the forces of rationalism and sound thinking. The premises have been purified of all assumptions made on the basis of sincerity, goodness, and affection. Visible events and things lose their relationships, becoming objects in meaningless lists of data. Birds fly because it is in their nature to fly; portraits smile and wink only to those whose senses deceive them. Friends ask because they have a purpose and interest in doing so. Even if it doesn't appear so in that particular conversation, it is only because they are cunning and know when to make their demands. Good timing is the secret to success in life and with people. Timing has no relationship to a magical moment in which time and place fall into harmony orchestrated by a self that faithfully maintains a severe vigilance for the sake of retaining those mad true moments, hoping for some victory in meaning:

"Why do you allow people to exploit you like this, Kimi? And then afterwards you're angry at them?" exclaimed her observant, prudent mother.

"No one exploits me. I give of my own free will, and I don't get angry."

"They consider you weak, they take what they want from you, and then when you're searching for someone to help you, you don't find anyone."

"People give what they're able to give."

"Except for you—you can give everything, isn't that so?"

Except for those moments the days were gray, not deserving that anyone live them. And in spite of the pain and the unbalanced, muddled imaginings, in spite of all the accusations—false or no—in the trial of the self, and all of the judgments that the self passes on itself and punishes: my death, mine, *ya ana*, liar you are, hypocrite! Arrogant, conceited, treacherous, neglectful, stupid, ugly, naïve, evil, reckless! You aren't good at anything, you're a Narcissus, you're not moved by others' wounds. You never extend a helping hand. Insolent, scornful—there's no hope to be had from you, and no forgiveness for you! You—only you—are the cause of all the evil in the world, all of its disasters, you alone are responsible, and you're afraid, as well—a coward with no strength at all.

Many images I snap. To many people I give those features and they embalm them in their albums on the surface-page of the Nile, at the foot of the Pyramids, in the garden of my grandmother's villa, my mother watering the plants on the balcony of our home, my father shaking hands with the President, my father between Nehru and Nkrumah. Latakia, Belgrade, Budapest, the beach resort in the summer of '67 . . . and the voices in my head rise, accusatory: You abandoned them. So I defend myself: They abandoned me, too. Who would acknowledge such a monstrous offspring, unlike all other children, one who hears voices and is afraid not to be afraid?

Doubt burns all images of affection. It exposes films suddenly to the tempestuous light of day and transforms mirror-eyes into stone. It makes humanity and treachery synonymous and teaches us not to believe anyone. We become smart and we joke: "You can . . . recall everything. Isn't that so? You . . . ."

READING LESSON

The professor is famous. He sits at a dais. He looks at me, searchingly, and says, "God is merciful to a person who knows his own worth." I am positive that he is directing his words to me. My own worth? I don't know my own worth? It's a paltry worth, and it decreases with every day that passes. But I almost succeeded. I almost got there. I almost let the layers peel off, the final skin drop. After the final layer goes, no one will see me, and it will no longer be in anyone's power to sting me with words and kill me. After the final layer, I will not be. Who asks about the essence of my worth? What is my worth? After the final layer, all wishes will come to fruition for the truthful, the steadfast, the just, the confident: I will be eradicated from those mirror-eyes. And no one will ever be forced to acknowledge, shamefacedly : "Yes, this wretched thing is the fruit of my ribs, and heritor of my legacy." Then I won't have to rebel, or to insist on my own existence, nor will I then regret such insistence: to spinning by night what I have unraveled by day, and the game will cease. "That girl, what overcame her to make her decline so?" they will inquire. They will ward off their guilt and inquire:

"What came over you? How did you get to be like this, without fear of no longer existing? In fact, what is this insistence on not existing?"

"I wanted to be . . . to live myself out, to try it."

"And so you never get anywhere, see? You never accomplish anything that way. You don't come to realize concrete reality. This self of yours is a thing you craft constantly. You carve it out, if need be, from nature, from the world around you."

"Yes, I've understood something of the sort from the start."

"Which start is that? You've started more times than one can count. And after every beginning you become like a spoiled child. You won't put up with the same toy for more than half a day."

"It's happened. I was yearning for something that has no core, no essence, and I haven't known how to recognize it. The whole world—that might be it. Either the whole world or nothing. How can a person long to be existence itself?"

102

"People long for many things that are impossible."

"Yes, and that is what I was training myself for. I was training myself, and that's what slowed me down for so long."

"Training does not remove the boundaries. You confused apples and oranges. Training is for the sake of excelling *within* the boundaries. Everyone knows that, everyone knows their limits, the boundaries that they can't exceed no matter how hard they try. Except for—"

"Except for those who are mad?"

"Yes. Except for those who are mad."

"And wizards and witches, to be precise, right, *grandmamma*?"

"Wizards and witches and poets and story writers and novelists and all chemists."

"And those who are wise, *grandmamma*?"

"Polite girls who listen to what they are told and do not stop to speak to the wolves in the forest."

"And you, why is your nose so big, *grandmamma*?"

"Go away, now, girl, you insolent child!"

She was supposed to say: "Because I'm ill, my dear," and then I would ask, "And why are your eyes so red, *grandmamma*?" And she would answer, "Because I'm ill, my girl," and so on until she pounces on Little Red Riding Hood to eat her, and then Little Red Riding Hood knows that her grandmother is not her grandmother and that the wolf has eaten her grandmother and disguised himself in her clothes so that he can eat her too, because her grandmother loved stories and believed—though she would never admit it to anyone else—that her kitchen was a chemistry laboratory that produced compounds to preserve health and to bring together all of her children.

When she said what she said I remembered that I had heard the likes of this often before. But at the time it dawned on me that the world *is* divided into two parts: sensible people who think the wizards and the witches are their enemies, and the wizards and the witches who fight the sensible people through words; and that the struggle goes on every day, and that since all days contain wizards and witches, all days are bewitched; and that there are days bewitched by white magic and other days by black magic; and that you find white magic in the spaces that words leave between the lines; and that black magic is the lines themselves, made by the words; and that the black days are those in which the evil sensible people succeed in preventing the wizards and the witches from filling the white pages; and that my grandmother was sensible. So I spent the night remaking the little girl in the red hood. I dressed her in black clothes because I did not like red, and because my grandmother had died.

Little Black Riding Hood lived in a hut on the banks of a great river, a clean and well-ordered hut, well cared for, with a lovely garden. Her grandmamma lived in a similar hut on the edges of the desert and yet the distance between the two huts was not great, because the desert was uncannily close to the river valley. That family had a secret that the mothers kept, not divulging it to anyone but the daughters. When a generation passed without the birth of a daughter, there hung over the women of the family a terrible fear that the secret would die with them before they could transmit it to another new daughter. And when Little Black Riding Hood reached the age at which it was possible to transmit this secret to her, her mother summoned her and told her that she would send her to her grandmamma on the edges of the desert, nearby, on a very important mission. Little Black Riding Hood did not ask questions, in the way that children do. Rather she went immediately to prepare herself for her departure.

That disturbed her mother, and she asked her daughter, "Don't you want to know the nature of that special mission?"

The daughter answered, "It's enough to know that it is special, and that you singled me out for it."

"It is special, and if I have charged you with it, it is not because you stand out from others in any way. Understand?"

That confused Little Black Riding Hood, because she had really believed that to go to her grandmother's cottage on a mission that her mother said was special meant that she, too, was special, and that this indeed distinguished her. She yielded to this obstacle, chastened, and was quiet, and listened to the rest of her mother's words.

"I will give you things to carry to your grandmamma. On the way, do not speak to anyone, do not answer anyone's greeting, and do not stop for any reason. And after you have given your grandmother the things that are with you, do not stay. Return at once, and do not stop on the way back, either, for any reason."

When Little Black Riding Hood reached her grandmother's place, having followed her mother's directions to the letter, she found the door wide open and she found herself unable to take another step. She sensed that if she went over the threshold, things would happen to her. Things of which she had no inkling. But she entered as if bewitched, and indeed her whole being was pervaded by a feeling that she had left one world behind her to enter a new world. She wondered to herself, "Then, is this death?"

At this point she heard the voice of her grandmother, coming to her from the kitchen. "Welcome, welcome, you arrived safely, my darling."

And she remembered; her mother had said as she bid her goodbye,

"The magic of words is in their tone. All music is in the timbre. And so is all the treachery."

SIRENS

The voices take on rainbow hues just as the speech billows the lines into waves and transforms them into melodies howling of death. The sirens whisper, beseeching, pleading. "Alone, you can, you alone of all people, you alone can rescue me, can help me. You only . . . alone."

Words, speech: Speech reels, spins thread out of itself, and weaves a larger space, and moves, and spreads . . . . Images beget images in a like process. The moment on the verge of quiet surrender . . . its lures are stronger than all the songs of the sirens together. In all tongues a strong bond seams the sirens and water: the bonds of water in the imaginations of men. And even when the sirens erupt from the fields—as they do in Egypt and Ireland—these are fields flooded by the water from rivulets and irrigation canals, or meadows squatting near a stream or a lake. And they love them to death. The death of men. The *naddaaha* with her siren call arises from the water, her long hair wet, clinging in places to her bare shoulders, and reaching as far as her buttocks. Her clothes divulge a bewitching beauty. She raises her hands to summon the passerby in a voice that will not brook resistance. This is her secret. Her secret is in her voice. The man strips off his clothes and runs behind her to the water and before he reaches her she has changed into a great owl whose laugh echoes through the still air over the lake. And he drowns.

The Danish siren is unlike any of her sisters, either those dwelling in the Aegean Sea or those who inhabit fields bewitched by the sun setting behind the villages of Egypt. The Danish siren lost her voice to a man's depredations, or she willingly gave it up so that the king of the seas would bestow on her a pair of feet with which she can step into a silvery sky-blue BMW and sit next to her handsome prince, smiling and waving from behind the car window to the people, without being able to utter a single word.

Only the one who lives in Warsaw, near the River Vistula, does not lure with a song that pillages the soul. Only she does not mock, nor renounce her weapons: the sword in one hand and the shield in the other, brandishing that steel, and watching. If the enemies pounce on her torn-apart country she leaps to the fight, and when she fights the music wells louder and all of the other sirens sing:

"*Tap tap tap*," "*Cockcarracarra*," "*mea culpa*," and "the beauty of the music" that robs your soul twice over.

From the memory on the wall: James Joyce has stopped, to stand still over my bed in Dublin. He puts his hands in the pockets of his loose trousers and looks at me, a look entirely good and affectionate, and then, like me, he looks towards a large placard on which is written: Silence: General Rehearsal: The Sirens of James Joyce.

From behind the placard has appeared a tall man, his black hair nearly touching his shoulders, with glints of silver here and there, his lips like those of Renaissance angels, wearing lightweight glasses with a frame the thickness of a golden wire. When he smiles his brown eyes smile in intelligent goodness.

When he reached my spot next to the sign, I spoke first, as I never had before.

"In sooth," you did not tell me. "What country, friend, are you from?"

He answered with a simplicity that captivated me.

"Ireland. I was born here. Ireland."

Then he added, after a pause in which he was getting out of the way of a bicycle that almost crushed his foot, "And you?"

The voices were louder than usual. They deafened me, and so I did not answer.

"Lord do not condemn us if we are forgetful, Lord, impose not on us that which we have not the strength to bear. Pardon us and absolve us."

"The Lord is merciful to those who know their true worth."

Welcome, welcome, you have finally arrived, my darling:

Finally, you have come to know that we are all of us born thus. And that your bewilderment was completely legitimate. How does one know to what family of sirens one belongs, if they have told one all of those tales, and then have forbidden one to write? How does one know to what languages one belongs if they have said, "Read in all languages," but then do not say, "Write!" Naturally, one's languages become a lexicon. And if languages become lexica, naturally, one denies—one becomes an apostate in—all languages. Denying, the scope of vision narrows, you become fanatic, narrowing your horizons to guard against completely fading away or disappearing into the whole. Will you not then have misgivings? All of us craft for ourselves those bells that protect us, and we huddle beneath them for a spell until we begin to suffocate—and then we shatter the bell. If we are lucky, we'll meet someone we can love, someone who will help us, and so the bonds are unraveled gently, and we do not notice until after we've noticed that we are breathing without watchful concern or worry.

James Joyce was still there, motionless before the sirens' sign. And he was saying, with a smile, "You're raving."

But I ignored what he said and posed him a question instead.

"When you were creating Molly Bloom, did you know that in Russia there are sirens who belong to the snow and ice? They come out from behind snowdrifts, and any man who looks at them turns to stone. Did you know that? And if the sirens look at the men, they turn into water. Did you know that?"

"Molly was Greek," answered James Joyce. "And Greece is the cradle of civilization."

I almost corrected him, but my mother had come in, interrupting our conversation. She did not notice him standing there, his hands still in his pockets.

"Come on, stop your silly staring at the ceiling! Come on, now, get up and come with me. Amna is ill too. She wants to see you are well. Go reassure her. Go and see her in her room. She is not strong enough to get out of bed. Come out of yourself for a moment. Show her that you care."

So I'm just feigning illness. Is that it? I just want to attract their attention. To what, exactly? All of those symptoms: "You have all the symptoms. It happens. Don't be afraid. Come, I'll take you to your home—I mean, I'll take you to your nation. My nation? Prithee sir tell me, what country is this? *Parallel, parallel.* The smell of oranges and the girls they kept from going to school in the land of Egypt, forbidding them to write. Fear. Doubt. Know that in the end, you are not worth so much as an onion. Listen to advice, and submit to punishment. Sky-blue silvery automobiles. Sensible people are strong. Stronger than all the wonderful magicians put together."

No, Amna, its me. *La ya Amna ana* . . . I am not ill, it is just that things happen that are mere words. I doubt things, and I'm sure of them, and I swing like that, between meanings that are good and honest, and meanings that are malevolent. The magic of tones pricks me and I cannot respond. Words swim and billow on the pages and take on meanings that contradict themselves from one moment to the next. Sometimes, on the leaves of paper, they appear heavily encumbered, pregnant, all but overflowing with a goodness enough to encompass all of humankind. Then, the very next moment the magic vanishes, and the wicked and the sensible prevail. It's like the music in voices. Do you understand?

Like your face in the mirror?

Exactly. How did you know?

All your life, you've spent your time staring into mirrors.

I turned and caught a glimpse of my face in the mirror above the dressing table.

The waters of the mirror are wavy, billowing, playing with my image like mercury, now I see it and now I don't. I hold tightly to the outward appearances of that existence, as if it really has been cut out of water. It slips from my eyes, glinting rays that harsh perception sent streaming, and I think back upon the echo of its bewitched entreaties. Its tone changes as it summons me:

You only, alone, can . . . you apart from all others . . . you only . . . can . . . save me . . . save us.

THE TRACE

I write, I erase. I write. What if someone reads these leaves of paper before they're . . . complete? Writing is never complete and yet people manage to read it! How can something be complete unless it dies? This is self-evident. Everything, as long as it is still alive, must be at some stage. Only when we die are we complete. Or when they kill us in words—our loved ones, so very determined to preserve our images just so, or in this form, or that. Or, we're made complete when we kill ourselves having so liked to claim that we were in this shape, or that, or that we still are. For there is something enticing about endings. The temptation to set in place the final endpoint, with our own hands, we kill ourselves, all by our selves. We choose not to be, as an alternative. Not being is more merciful surely. For being demands that we never end . . . never. Being demands that we erase and return to writing and life once again, a writing and a life that might be.

Modern Arabic Literature
from the American University in Cairo Press

Ibrahim Abdel Meguid *Birds of Amber*
No One Sleeps in Alexandria • *The Other Place*
Yahya Taher Abdullah *The Mountain of Green Tea*
Leila Abouzeid *The Last Chapter*
Yusuf Abu Rayya *Wedding Night*
Ahmed Alaidy *Being Abbas el Abd*
Idris Ali *Dongola: A Novel of Nubia*
Ibrahim Aslan *The Heron* • *Nile Sparrows*
Alaa Al Aswany *The Yacoubian Building*
Hala El Badry *A Certain Woman* • *Muntaha*
Salwa Bakr *The Wiles of Men*
Hoda Barakat *Disciples of Passion* • *The Tiller of Waters*
Mourid Barghouti *I Saw Ramallah*
Mohamed El-Bisatie *Clamor of the Lake* • *Houses Behind the Trees*
A Last Glass of Tea • *Over the Bridge*
Fathy Ghanem *The Man Who Lost His Shadow*
Randa Ghazy *Dreaming of Palestine*
Gamal al-Ghitani *Zayni Barakat*
Tawfiq al-Hakim *The Prison of Life*
Yahya Hakki *The Lamp of Umm Hashim*
Bensalem Himmich *The Polymath* • *The Theocrat*
Taha Hussein *The Days* • *A Man of Letters* • *The Sufferers*
Sonallah Ibrahim *Cairo: From Edge to Edge* • *The Committee* • *Zaat*
Yusuf Idris *City of Love and Ashes*
Denys Johnson-Davies *The AUC Press Book of Modern Arabic Literature*
Under the Naked Sky: Short Stories from the Arab World
Said al-Kafrawi *The Hill of Gypsies*
Sahar Khalifeh *The Inheritance*
Edwar al-Kharrat *Rama and the Dragon* • *Stones of Bobello*